Connie Morris has always been something of a pushover. She does whatever her boss tells her, whatever her husband tells her, whatever her best friend tells her. No wonder she is confused when a dream lover appears who has something new to tell her: Relax. Take it easy. Let me do the work.

When Connie finally gives in to her fantasy man, the sex is better than anything she's ever experienced in her life. But as she basks in the afterglow, a letter arrives for her husband, with proof that Connie cheated on him.

How can this be? Her affair was one in mind only. But nobody believes that possibility—nobody, that is, until Connie finds Joseph. Joseph understands that there was something more sinister to Connie's dream encounters. With Joseph's help, Connie strengthens her mental powers until she can block the attacks from the dream lover, track him herself, and vanquish him.

But along the way, she and Joseph find love of their own—and this happens outside of Connie's fantasies and in her own reality.

# THE ESP AFFAIR

alison tyler

*an erotic romance*

First Magic Carpet Inc. edition May 2002

Published in 2002

Manufactured in th United States of America
Published by Magic Carpet Books

Magic Carpet Books
PO Box 473
New Milford, CT 06776

Library of Congress Cataloging in Publication Data

The ESP Affair by Alison Tyler
ISBN 0-937609-45-5

cover design: stella by design contact: stellabydesign@aol.com

interior design: stella by design and Scott Friedlander

For SAM, with love.

*By night we're hurled
by dreams, each one, into a several world.*
—Robert Herrick

# PROLOGUE

Connie sprawled naked on a tropical beach, her long-limbed body partially submerged in the warm, aqua water. Sunlight shone brilliantly on the hot golden sand, making the beach sparkle as if dusted with slivers of pure diamonds. Palm trees bent lazily in the summer breeze, their dark emerald fronds dipping in a silent dance.

He was with her. His strong arms surrounded her slender waist, pulling her into a tight embrace. She could feel his hard muscled body, demanding as it pressed against her own from behind. One of his hands trailed down her concave belly, his fingers tickling her skin. With finesse, he slid his hand between her supple thighs, then carefully ran his fingertips up and down. With each touch—and each thrust—he brought her closer to that tantalizing finish line, a magical place where they would both melt together into the passion of sizzling summer bliss.

Oh, yes, she had almost reached it.

"Connie—you done in there?"

If only Ron would shut up.

Fiercely, she tried to force herself back into the erotic mood. Closing her clear green eyes again, she repeated to herself, "Beach. I'm relaxing on a beautiful beach," but although she used the words like a mantra, Connie still couldn't come. She wanted to— desperately. Her knowledgeable fingers made their standard slow rotations against her silky wet skin, stroking at the perfect pace.

Yes, just like that—

With her other hand, she caressed her small round breasts, flicking her thumb against one nipple, then the other, until both stood erect, like pebbles polished smooth by ocean waves.

"Connie! Are you coming?"

Nope. Not anymore.

The rich scent of her "Mango Mania" bubble bath surrounded her, and she slid a little bit lower in the large, sunken claw-foot tub, feeling the water lap at her skin like the gentle kiss of the surf. She bent her knees and placed one foot on either side of the silver faucet, then sent a startling spray cascading in a makeshift waterfall over the split of her body. But nothing worked. The pressure from Ron had thrown off her delicate timing, and she knew from past experience that she might as well climb out of the bath and dry herself off with one of the pastel towels from the nearby wicker cabinet.

Now her husband was calling for her to hurry up—he needed to jump in the shower and wash away the sweat from this evening's energetic racquetball game. This image finally evaporated what remained of her sensual mood.

"Taking a bubble bath" was Connie's quaint little code for wanting to luxuriate in some sensual solo time, but after four years of marriage, Ron still hadn't gotten that. And Connie had never bothered to explain.

# BOOK ONE

*Art thou poor, yet hast thou golden slumbers?*
—Thomas Dekker

# CHAPTER ONE

Ron Morris struck a pose in front of his full-length closet mirror. He turned sideways, checking out his handsome profile, then winked casually at his reflection. The recently acquired gray streaks in his thick, black curls gave him a distinguished air that was further enhanced by a year-round, California tan. His lean body was well built from hours of basketball and swimming at the exclusive North Beach Athletic Club. It wasn't just vanity that made him work out. He had a good reason for keeping fit: Deleen.

Thinking about her made his face break into a boyish grin. Her image did more than simply make him smile—he got a hard-on solely from picturing her, remembering how well they moved together. Closing his eyes, he called up a fleeting flashback of Deleen in her lavender bikini, beckoning to him from the balcony of an ocean facing Hawaiian hotel suite. They'd made love in the easy swing-and-sway of the white cloth hammock, feeling the heat of the late afternoon sun warming their bodies.

Behind him on the bed, Connie sighed. Ron tensed at the sound and opened his eyes into a guilty squint. Was she watching him fantasize about his lover? Would she know what his expression meant if she saw it? Cautiously, he looked over his shoulder to make sure that his wife hadn't caught him admiring himself, or seen the longing in his dark hazel eyes. With relief, he realized that she hadn't. Although she sat propped upright against the wooden headboard holding onto a tattered paperback novel, Connie was breathing deeply, already fast asleep. Ron took the opportunity to study her unobserved. She possessed a good figure and a lovely face, yet her appearance no longer captivated him— that power was held by his secret girlfriend who lived 3,000 miles away.

Quietly, Ron opened the closet door. The interior looked like an advertisement for a space organizer system—everything in its assigned place, precisely hung or neatly folded. He chose several hand-tailored shirts, an Italian sweater, and two brightly colored imported silk ties. After one last reassuring glance toward his sleeping wife, he reached into the back of his sock drawer and located a small, cobalt blue velvet box. This he sandwiched between the shirts and swiftly carried the stack to his suitcase.

With Deleen's gift now safely hidden, the tightness in his broad shoulders left him. He stepped to the bed and removed the book from Connie's grasp, frowning at the image of the attractive couple embracing on the cover—blonde bimbo and dark-haired surfer dude. It was so cliché. He and Deleen had lived the real thing, with Connie naively believing that he was off on one of his many business trips.

Feeling nosy, he turned to the page she'd been reading and skimmed a few lines of description: *Rick took his shirt off slowly, revealing his strong chest, arms rippled with muscles from his stint as a longshoreman. While Jenni watched, Rick slid out of his faded Levis, revealing a pair of turquoise-and-white swim trunks. After tossing the jeans onto the colorful beach blanket, he headed out to the surf with his board under one arm. When would he turn around and notice her? She'd been standing in the shade of the palm tree for several minutes, posed carefully in her petal pink striped bikini.*

*Come on, Rick, she mentally pleaded. Turn around. Turn around, now!*

Grimacing, Ron set the book face down on the wooden nightstand, further cracking the spine. Romance novels weren't his style. He preferred reality to fantasy any day. Why live in a dream world when you could go after what you really wanted. He glanced at Connie, whose full lips moved silently in her sleep. For a moment, he pondered the subject of her dreams. Then he smiled at the absurdity of his curiosity. Nothing Connie could possibly dream about would interest him. Just look at how she spent her time: reading romance novels, worrying about her elementary school students, and talking to her brainless—and often braless—friend Marla. Knowing his wife as well as he did, he was certain that any after-dark feature playing on the movie screen of her mind couldn't be very exciting.

He was wrong.


Connie stood alone in a circle of rippling golden light. From somewhere in the surrounding darkness, a voice crooned, "Connie, I'm glad you're finally here."

She peered into the gloom, then called out, "I can't see you."

A man, tall and lean, entered the lit area. He wore faded 501s and a blue oxford-cloth shirt. His fluid movements made her guess him to be in his late twenties, the same age as she was. Because his face was hidden in shadow no matter how he moved, it was impossible to tell for sure.

"Who are you?" she asked.

Rather than answer, he strode forward, took hold of one of her hands and brought it to his lips, softly kissing the inside of her wrist. His mouth lingered there for a moment, and she stayed still, paying attention to the way her body responded automatically to his touch. But after several seconds, she instinctively pulled away, moving several steps from his reach.

"Come closer, Connie."

"First, tell me your name."

"Think of me as someone who wants to be with you."

Again he closed the distance between them, and now he placed his palm against the small of her back, turning her the way a well-trained dancer might steer his partner. A blue-and-white striped mattress lay in the center of the room, only a few feet away. Connie's mind felt hazy and vague, but she was fairly certain that the circle of light had been empty only a moment earlier.

"Let's get more comfortable," the man said, steering her toward the bare, makeshift bed. There were no sheets or pillows, nothing but the utilitarian mattress. Connie stiffened at his touch, frightened for the first time. She had that odd sensation that she was dreaming—and that she *knew* she was dreaming—yet the scenario felt decidedly real. She saw how highly polished the wood floor was and noticed the way the shadows moved on the mattress, as she and the man grew closer. Were details that specific found in ordinary dreams? She couldn't remember.

"I won't hurt you," the man said reassuringly.

*Then what are you going to do?* She wasn't sure if she'd spoken her feelings aloud, but he responded as if she had.

"I'm going to make you feel good. Better than you have in a long time."

Was he reading her mind?

"Don't be afraid," he said, beckoning to her. She felt a natural inclination to go toward him and into his waiting embrace. From deep within herself, she wanted to.

"I'm married," she whispered.

"That bond means nothing here." From his tone, she thought that he must have been smiling, although his features remained hidden no matter how hard she tried to see his face.

"I'm *married*," she repeated louder, twirling the platinum band of her wedding ring nervously on her finger. His pull on her intensified, but she held her ground.

"In this place, you are absolutely free. Everything you've ever fantasized about can come true." He paused, then added, "And Connie—"

She looked at him.

"It's going to be so nice."

At his words, she found that she wanted to explore with a stranger the thoughts that gave her the most pleasure in bed. But she couldn't. She was a good girl, wasn't she?

"Are you?" he asked. "Are you really? Wouldn't you have more fun being a bad girl for once, Connie? Being really, truly bad."

"I can't," she whispered. "Ron will be angry."

"Ron?" The man spat the single word contemptuously, making the name sound like an obscenity. At his sudden burst of anger Connie turned and rushed away, disappearing into the inky darkness.

When Connie opened her eyes, she saw her husband carefully folding his freshly ironed boxer shorts and placing them into his leather suitcase, one after the other. Ron enjoyed the puzzle-like game of making everything fit. His shirts were in two matching stacks, and his rolled socks filled out the corners of the suitcase. When he noticed she was awake, he said, "It's late, Con. Go back to sleep."

"Are you coming to bed?"

"In a second. I'm almost done."

So tired, Connie settled down beneath the rumpled covers again, got comfortable against her pillow, and shut her eyes.

Although the man stood exactly where she'd left him, the room was different, as if scenery movers had been busy in her absence, filling the stage. Now, a multitude of colors flickered across the floor as if a crystal chandelier hung overhead, just out of sight. The mattress sat on a bed with a fancy wooden frame, intricate curls forming the head and footboards. It was exactly like the one that had stood in her grandmother's house during Connie's youth.

"I've been waiting, Connie. I knew you'd be back." He walked to the edge of the bed and sat down. "Come here," he said, patting an area at his side, but Connie didn't move, regarding him with an openly questioning stare.

"My grandfather made that bed."

"He was a master craftsman."

"How could you know what it looked like? It was destroyed in a fire years ago. There aren't even any pictures of it left."

"*You* know what it looked like, Connie. A photo-quality image of it is embedded in your mind. And I know everything you know." He explained this patiently, as one might when talking to a child.

"That's impossible. You couldn't."

"But I do," the man said evenly. He rose again and walked over to her, standing at her side. Then he put his hand under her chin, lifting her face to his. His features were blurred, as if she were seeing them through a heavy gauze, but she caught the strong shape of his jaw line now, and could see the depth of his dark blue eyes. "I know so many things, Connie." He brought his lips against her ear, and her skin tingled at the warmth of his breath. "I know your innermost thoughts, your secret desires. And I am going to fulfill each one, slowly, so slowly. I'll treat you the way you deserve to be treated, Connie. The way you yearn for a man to touch you."

He held her in his arms, cradling the curves of her hips in his hands. When she felt his sex throbbing against her through his jeans, she recoiled from him as violently as if he'd slapped her.

"I'm being sweet with you, Connie. And I know that you like it. I *know*—"

He started toward her again, but she retreated, saying, "I'm going."

"Stay here." His voice, although still husky with need, now had a harsh undertone.

"No."

He had his arms around her quickly, and he held her more tightly this time, capturing her from behind so that she couldn't move. He kissed her shoulders, and when she began to tremble at his touch, he kissed her more passionately.

"Please," she said, her voice catching, on the edge of tears. "You have to stop. This is wrong. I've never been unfaithful to my husband."

The man lifted her long hair in one hand and brought his lips against the soft down at the back of her neck. He kissed in a line there, at that most sensitive spot. As she shivered, he whispered, "We can do this easy, or we can do this hard."

"I'll scream."

He said nothing.

"You don't think  I really will, do you?"

"I know you will, Connie. I already told you. I know everything you know. Every single thing." He slid his hands up her bare arms, digging his fingers firmly into her tender skin.

She screamed.

Ron closed his expensive leather suitcase and looked over at his slumbering wife. Her lips were slightly parted, but no sound came out.

In the bed, in the circle of light, Connie stopped screaming. The man was next to her on the blanket now, his hands roaming freely over her body. "I don't know you," she said. "You're not Ron."

"Thank God for that."

He bent his head to kiss her lips, and she felt herself responding, her hips shifting uncontrollably on the soft down comforter. It had been such a long time since she'd felt craved in such a sexy manner.

"Like this, Connie," he whispered, "Just open your mouth a little and answer my tongue. You want to. I know you do. Let yourself go."

He kissed her again, his lips pressed against her own, his hands moving up and into her sandy-blonde hair. Breathlessly, she kissed him back, hearing her heart pounding in her ears at a rapid pace. Just as she found herself wanting more, the man pulled away slightly, whispering, "Now, isn't that good?"

A pale, cotton-candy pink flush colored her cheeks. She felt warm all over.

"Ron doesn't kiss you like that. Not anymore. Just a peck on the lips when he arrives home from one of his many 'business' trips. A little pat on your gorgeous ass when he rolls over next to you in bed. Don't you miss it, Connie? Don't you miss being with someone? Someone whose solitary desire is to make you feel good?" His voice grew even softer, and she had to lean forward to hear him. "And you can bank on this, Miss Constance Elizabeth Morris. I'm going to make you feel so good." He had her wrists firmly in one of his hands, and he drew them high over her head, stretching her body upward, elongating her. He kissed her again like this, with her his captive, and she felt as if she might actually faint from the pleasure.

With his free hand, the man ran his fingers lightly over her firm breasts, then began to undo the fine lace tie at the top of her nightgown. "Now, let me see how beautiful you really are."

As he peeled open her nightgown, the light in the room shifted, changing easily with the mood. The enchanting ambiance of candlelight flickered over Connie's skin. She felt beautiful as the man moved slightly back from her, staring at her in silent awe. Her long hair draped over her shoulders, and her body remained nestled in the fabric of the nightgown.

"Oh, Connie," the man sighed, reaching forward.

At his touch, she fought within herself, torn between her mounting desire to give in and a nagging unease at how much she was enjoying the situation. She'd never cheated before. Not that other men had tried to flirt with her since she'd first gotten together with Ron. Connie was definitely pretty. But she'd ignored every advance. She simply wasn't the type to act on that sort of situation.

When the man moved aside so that she could undress, her conscience won over her libido and she broke away and moved off the bed.

"Silly girl," he called after her, not bothering to get up. "You'll be back." Now he laughed confidently, and his laughter held a knowing sound. "And I'll be waiting."

Connie woke to the steady rhythm of Ron's snores. His arm was thrown heavily across her body, anchoring her to the bed. For a moment, she considered waking him and describing her unsettling dream. Then she reconsidered. He was taking an early flight in the morning. It would be unfair to make him lose sleep over her fear about a phantom lover. Besides, most likely he'd tease her for being overly sexed-up, say that she'd been hanging out with the bad-influence of Marla for too long. She didn't need to hear any of his snide comments right now.

Blinking in the semi-darkness, she tried to gain control of her thoughts. Despite knowing what Ron's comments would be, the dream had felt so real. Yes, she'd pushed the man away in her mind, but the thought of giving in to him had truly excited her. The way the man held her and touched her turned her on more than any of her current fantasies. Connie thought of sensually stroking herself right now as she replayed the exotic scene in her head. A quick climax would undoubtedly relax her mind and help her to fall asleep. Cautiously, she slid her hand down her body. The motion disturbed Ron, who muttered something unintelligible into his goose-down pillow and rolled away from her.

This wasn't going to work.

Resigned, Connie sat up, swung out of bed, and tiptoed to her closet. Unlike Ron's, her closet was a complete disaster area, far more clothes on the floor than on hangers. She dug out her favorite blue flannel bathrobe and groped her way down the stairs. The kitchen was bathed in an alien glow from the stove's digital clock, its green numbers changing from 1:17 to 1:18 as Connie watched. Despite the fact that she had an early faculty meeting in the morning, and knew she'd be a mess without sleep, she turned on the automatic coffee machine. She wanted to clear her head. Perhaps the cozy smell of French Roast would lift her spirits.

As she waited for the coffee to brew, she caught a glimpse of her worried face in the chrome surface of the toaster and forced a smile. What had the man called her? "Silly girl." He had that right. "Snap out of it, Connie," she chided herself, using the same stern teacher voice she employed with her students when she wanted their complete attention. "This is the real world. Big girls aren't afraid of the dark." She carried a steaming mug of coffee into the living room and snuggled up on the rose-patterned sofa. Elmer, her orange-striped tabby cat, sauntered in from the dining room and crawled into Connie's lap. Happy to have company he kneaded her leg with outstretched claws, and she absentmindedly stroked his knobby head until he began to purr.

Ron's airline tickets rested on the coffee table. Slowly, so as not to disturb the sleeping cat, Connie leaned over and pulled the itinerary from the envelope. SFO to Washington DC to Atlanta to Miami and back to San Francisco's International Airport. She felt exhausted just looking at the whirlwind schedule, but she knew from experience that Ron gained energy from that kind of a go-go-go routine.

She replaced the paper and considered finding something to occupy her mind. *A Beach-Town Fling*, the romance she'd been reading that evening, was still upstairs on her bedside table. But the bookcase across the room held several novels she'd been meaning to get to all summer. Should she move Elmer and grab the most recent *New York Times* bestseller? Or maybe pick up the exercise book Marla had loaned her? Suddenly, the effort of simply standing and taking a dozen steps seemed too much. Her vision blurred.

A bouquet of fragrant purple violets stood in a blue glass vase on a table next to the bed. Covering the shiny wood floor was a sumptuous-looking pure white rug that felt deliciously soft beneath Connie's bare feet. Rich, brocade tapestries were suspended impossibly in mid-air around the bed, making the space seem cozy and intimate, even though the darkness was just beyond their fringe. Connie's all-time favorite Bob Dylan tune played softly from a source she couldn't locate. The man sat upright on the edge of the bed, singing along with his own lyrics. "Come on, Connie. Why don't you lay across my big, wooden bed—"

Dylan continued solo as the man said, "Stay, with me. Stop running." He motioned to a spot next to him. Connie remained where she stood, paralyzed by her conflicting emotions.

"You've always loved this song, right?" He didn't wait for her to respond. "I think it's one of his greatest, too, although I've always been more of a Zeppelin man myself." He held out his hand to her, and again she felt herself drawn to him, as if by an unseen force. She took a deep breath, allowing herself to be pulled toward the bed in slow, halting steps. When she reached him, the man took her into his arms, caressing her hair in the same soothing way she had pet Elmer. The stranger supported Connie between his legs, and she settled into his embrace, his steady hand hypnotizing her.

"Are you ready, baby?" His voice had a soft croon to it. Easy, comforting. At his words, her will vaporized, giving her body the freedom to respond on its own. She pressed closer to him, as he continued to talk to her.

"I'll tell you a secret, Connie." He paused for a long, seductive beat, then asked, "Can you keep a secret?" She didn't answer, but he continued as if she had. "I know what you think about when you and Ron have sex. While he's doing you, pushing forward in the standard, boring missionary style, you aren't really there. Sure, your body is on the bed beneath him. But your mind is far away, off in the stratosphere. You close your eyes and visualize one of those handsome guys from your romance novels making love to you instead of Ron—someone who knows what a woman really needs. A man who undresses you slowly, gently, making you ache. Making you beg. You want to beg, don't you?"

"Stop—"

But he drove on whispering in a voice so forceful that she felt the words burned into her mind, glittering there as if on fire. "I know what you want."

This was a test. If he really did know—if he *could* honestly guess her different desires—then let him tell her right now. He could describe each fantasy, or at least one treasured fantasy. He could prove it. Holding her breath, she waited for him to continue.

"Oh, baby," he whispered. "You know I'm telling the truth, don't you? You can feel it deep inside yourself. But you want me to spell it out, don't you? You want proof."

In spite of herself, Connie nodded.

"You've got such dirty thoughts in that pretty head of yours. They make you feel naughty, don't they?"

She wouldn't say a word.

He tilted his head back, as if he had to choose from a list of many different options. "Let's see, Connie. Let me see exactly what it is that gives you pleasure in bed, when you're playing make-believe games in your mind. You want to be free with yourself the way your best friend Marla is. Wasn't that terribly kinky of her to go get a tattoo to surprise her boyfriend? That idea turned you on, didn't it?"

Connie nodded, but didn't speak.

"She chose the perfect spot, an area on her body that not many people will get to see unless they're invited to a private viewing. And then she waited for Zach to find that little heart on the curve of her hip. You liked that."

Again, Connie nodded. She had been intrigued by the idea, and the way the scene had all worked out for Marla—Zachary loving the tattoo and the treasure hunt of finding it. But it wasn't something she could turn into a reality. She could just hear Ron's displeasure as she revealed a piece of skin art to her husband. "You got a what? Where? Without me?"

"What else?" the dream lover continued. "You're a secret exhibitionist. Deep down, you'd love an audience to watch you make love. People all around, staring, seeing. Getting turned-on from watching you." He held up one hand, ticking off the items with his fingers. "You think dressing up in sexy clothes would be the ultimate aphrodisiac...and even more exciting would be having a man take them off of you. Drawing a silken robe away from your body. Sliding down a pair of fishnet stockings. Undoing the long satin ties on a black velvet corset."

Connie realized she was holding her breath, listening so intently, desperate to hear what he had to say.

"You could never tell Ron about the things you think about. The things you crave. Christ, the man is so dense about what you need that he can't even leave you alone long enough in the tub for you to properly get off." He hesitated, and she felt that he was smiling at her. "You pretend to be such a good girl on the surface, don't you?

But deep down you and I both know what a bad girl you are, Connie, and you know just what happens to bad girls, don't you?"

Oh, he did know. He'd seen it all spelled out clearly in her thoughts. Her knees would have given out if he hadn't been holding her. "You're doing something to my head," she said. "You're trying to control me." Her voice was a whimper.

"I'm trying to make love to you."

"I won't be forced this way. I won't—"

"You don't have a choice," he said, still speaking in that same, soothing tone. "You'll do exactly what I say. Everything I say. And you know why?" This time, he didn't wait for her response. "You'll do it because deep down inside, Connie, you want to do what I say."

"No!" She pushed him fiercely and ran.

# CHAPTER TWO

"And then...?" Marla Cooper demanded, her gleaming blue eyes opened wide in hungry anticipation. This was exactly the type of story that she most loved, but she'd never heard anything even remotely like these titillating tidbits from her best friend. Marla was generally the one to regale Connie with tales of erotic exploits — making love in the dressing room of the store she owned, doing it on a glass elevator in one of San Francisco's towering hotels — while Connie was known for keeping bedroom issues in the bedroom. She didn't often share her most private personal thoughts. Not even with Marla.

"Then nothing," Connie said emphatically. "Nothing at all." She put the last bite of her pasta salad into her mouth, chewed, swallowed, and followed it with a sip of chilled white wine.

"Nothing?" echoed Marla, shaking her ginger-hued curls in amazement. When she moved her head, her beaded silver earrings tinkled musically like wind chimes. Two college-aged boys, walking by the outdoor cafe, glanced at Marla. Next to Connie's prudish teacher's outfit of a plaid jumper and navy blue turtleneck, Marla looked like a runway model, absolutely ravishing in a form-fitting white sundress and thin crocheted sweater. The young men sent suggestive smiles in her direction. It was obvious from their sly expressions exactly what they were thinking—sexual sandwich. Marla ignored the appreciative stares, much too intent on Connie's story to allow herself to respond. "Come on," she urged, "there had to be more than just a hug and a kiss."

"I told you. I broke free."

Marla snorted. "You woke up."

"It wasn't like waking up. It was more like escaping."

"That's right," Marla said, rolling her eyes dramatically. "You were *escaping* from this romantic, good-looking guy—"

"I don't know if he was good-looking," Connie said, "I couldn't see his face."

"In a sexy situation like that, the face really isn't always the most important thing to see."

"You're disgusting," Connie said, laughing in spite of herself. "But it doesn't matter what any part of him looked like. I'm married. Ron was sleeping right there in bed next to me while this man was doing his seducing games. Was I supposed to just have sex with this dream lover while I was lying on the mattress next to my husband?" Connie looked down at her wedding band and diamond engagement ring. The sunlight caught in the gem, sending a multitude of tiny rainbows shooting across the white tablecloth.

"You're aware that threesomes can be a turn-on, right? A lot of women fantasize about doing two men at once." Marla glanced over her shoulder, indicating the two well-built youths disappearing around the corner.

Connie looked shocked. "I'm not one of them. One man at a time is plenty for me—"

"Wait, Con." Marla held up her hand. "Were you trying out that cool new dream-sex technique before you went to bed?"

"The what?"

"I just read about it in the latest issue of *Cosmopolitan* magazine. There's this method of mentally preparing yourself for a night to remember. You do it right before you go to sleep, by concentrating all of your thoughts on your—" Marla looked down, indicating the region between her well-toned thighs. She had her own choice X-rated words for this center of attention, but she chose a term specifically for Connie's sensitive nature. "On your 'special place.' You think hard about it, visualizing yourself growing more and more aroused. You can even talk to it, if that helps—"

"Right," Connie said. "I can just see that. Me talking to my you-know-what while Ron calls in the nice men wearing white coats."

Marla continued as if Connie hadn't interrupted. "Supposedly, when you do go to sleep, you have these intensely sexual dreams. Erotic images flash through your mind one right after another. Your subconscious plays everything out for you, like some personally directed porno movie. Maybe you created this dream man without even meaning to. I mean, what did this man say to you that couldn't really have been your own thoughts in disguise?"

Connie hesitated. She didn't really like the sound of what Marla was suggesting. It made her feel as if she'd been unfaithful to Ron. "He knew all of my fantasies," she said. "Every one of them." She'd edited the story a bit before telling Marla about her dream. Now she recalled the different possibilities the man had described for her and she felt her cheeks start to flush just at the memory.

"But that doesn't prove anything—you could simply have invented this image of a sexy man who could take care of you the way you most want who could do in bed the things you most crave, the things your husband doesn't—"

Suddenly, Connie held up her hand. "Shh. Stop talking."

"What's wrong?" Marla whispered.

Connie leaned forward and mouthed, "Our waiter's been eavesdropping. I think he heard everything I said."

Marla swiveled her head to study the waiter. He was dark-haired and slender, in his mid-twenties, not bad-looking at all. Although he pretended that he hadn't been listening, a tiny grin gave him away. It also enhanced his Mediterranean appeal. After giving Marla time to size him up, the waiter approached the table.

"Anything else, ladies? We've got a wonderful no-flour brownie today." As if the statement might need additional translation, he added. "No flour means 'all chocolate.'"

"Let's get it," urged Marla. She loved exploring sensuality in all forms—clothing, food, art, and sex.

"I'm trying to be good—"

"A few bites won't show."

"Don't tempt me."

"You really ought to try this dessert," the waiter piped in. "Our chef inherited the recipe from his great-grandmother. It's been in the family for years. You'll never taste anything like it anywhere else."

"One piece, two forks," Marla ordered. The waiter hurried away.

"I'm not having any," Connie insisted.

"Boy, are you tough on yourself. No dessert, no dream lover."

"Even if I had wanted to do it with this weird phantom guy—which I didn't—I'm telling you that Ron was right there."

"Don't talk crazy. Ron wasn't there. This encounter was in your head, not your bed. Even old married couples are entitled to privacy in their dreams. Or so I've heard."

"I would have run away from him even if I were single. The whole scene was too strange for me. I like things nice and simple—a little romance, a little sweet-talking. I mean, I didn't ask this character to come and seduce me by hypnosis."

The waiter, bringing the dessert, caught Connie's last phrase. After setting down the plate, he lingered a moment, obviously hoping for another hot tidbit.

"We're ready for the bill," said Connie, using her most unfriendly tone. The man let his shoulders droop dramatically to signal his disappointment, then placed the bill on the edge of the table. After taking a bite of the pie and making "mmmm" noises, Marla pushed the plate toward her friend. Connie shook her head.

"Don't be such a kill-joy."

Connie eyed the dessert, shrugged helplessly, and took a bite. Then she slid the plate back over. Although she was uncomfortable continuing the conversation, she couldn't stop herself from asking Marla another question. "Maybe you are right. Maybe I just made this guy up. But have you ever had a dream like that?"

"What do you mean?"

"A dream that was so real that it just didn't feel like you were dreaming at all."

"Sure," Marla shrugged. "I think everyone has. You wake up in a cold sweat and then look around and see that you're still in your own bedroom. And you shake it off. Think about it, Connie. When you opened your eyes, you were still safe in your own bed, weren't you?"

Connie nodded.

Between bites, Marla teased, "But if your mystery man *does* visit again, and if you decide to give him the permanent brush-off, forward him over to me. At the moment, I could use a hot companion. Even a make-believe lover would be welcome."

"I thought everything was fine between you and Zach," Connie said as she studied the check. "That story you told me about showing off your brand-new tattoo for him was intense." She fished into her handbag, then placed a few bills on the table. Marla matched the amount.

"Things *were* fine," corrected Marla as they got up from the table and headed down the sidewalk. "But he's canceled on me for our last two dates. Both times, he claimed rehearsals went late, but I just don't know."

"So it's over with him?"

"He promised to come by later tonight. I won't believe it until I see him standing on my porch, begging me in that cute southern drawl of his to let him in. You know what musicians are like. Especially, lead guitarists. No concept of time when they're not on stage." She paused. "Check with me after ten."

"This evening, I'm checking with no one. I slept for maybe twenty minutes last night. Ron's on another one of his whirlwind business trips, where he lives on coffee and visits three time zones in a day. I'm going to spend his absence paying back that sleep debt."

"If your mystery lover doesn't return."

They'd arrived at Connie's silver Volvo, packed to the top with books, toys, puzzles, a "Wild Thing" doll, and other tools of the teacher's trade. As Connie squeezed herself in, she said, "I never have the same dream twice. And even if he *did* come back, I'd be too busy sorting through all this stuff. So unless he finds it erotic to help me wade through my lesson plans, he's out of luck. School starts in less than two weeks, and this year I'm teaching first grade. All new assignments."

"I thought you liked third grade."

"Yeah," Connie said, "But the principal was desperate, and you know how I am. Can't say 'no.'"

Connie blew Marla a kiss and pulled away from the curb.

*I sure do*, Marla thought to herself.

# CHAPTER THREE

"Pretty thing," Zachary said, looking up and down at Marla's gleaming silver nightgown and long sheer robe. "Did you get all fancy like that for me?"

"Actually, I got all fancy for my other boyfriend, but he canceled on me. Again. Three strikes and he's out. So I guess you'll have to do." Marla couldn't say the words without smiling. She was pleased that Zach had surprised her at her apartment, washing away all of her doubts about him simply by showing up.

"I don't buy it," Zachary said, "Who'd cancel on a pretty girl like you?" He ran one hand under Marla's chin, lifting her head so that he could look into her large blue eyes. Just the brush of his fingers sent dangerous shivers through her. "I think you got all spiffed up like that just for me," he continued. "What makes me so special?" He spoke in a low voice, his body right next to hers.

"You're flattering yourself," Marla laughed.

"No," he teased. "I'm flattering you—"

"Is that what you call this type of conversation?"

"It's been too long," he said, standing above her, "you just don't remember." As he spoke, he slid off his leather jacket, and then opened his shiny black shirt one button at a time. He performed a funky strip tease, showing off the colorful tattoos on his forearms that danced when he flexed. A green and blue snake lay coiled around his left forearm, and a pair of crimson lips blew a kiss from his right shoulder.

Marla settled back on her large canopied bed to enjoy the show. She loved the occasions when she and Zach took their time, stretching out a mood. There was no need to rush—they had all night. Zachary hummed along as he did his clumsy bump and grind. His black engineer boots were next. He pulled them off while leaning against the wall, then stood upright to undo the button-fly of his dyed black 501s. With his jeans off he posed, hands on his hips in a model's stance. Then he jutted his chin toward her and said, "Go get that plaid skirt, baby."

"Which skirt?"

"You know, the one I like. Short and sweet. Showing off those race-horse legs of yours."

"The school girl skirt," she said, correctly naming the one he desired.

"Oh yeah," Zachary sighed. "That, along with some little white socks, and your high-heeled patent leather shoes."

"Sounds as if we're going to be playing dress-up," she said, coyly.

He nodded, encouraging her.

"What am I supposed to be?"

"You're going to dress as a bad, bad school girl. And I'll say this—with you, Marla, it's not really a costume. You might even have to come in to see the principal after class today."

She eyed him carefully, head tilted back, long eyelashes half lowered as she appraised him. "For a principal, you've sure got a lot of tattoos," she said finally, laughing. Her response won her a scowl, and he lunged for the bed, easily capturing her in his strong embrace. Marla continued to laugh as Zachary's relentless fingers roamed over her body. He tickled her until she collapsed into a fit of serious giggles, and then left her alone for a moment to calm herself.

"I don't think I need any costumes tonight," she told him, ready already.

Zachary knew what she meant, and he pulled open her satin robe so that it framed her stunning body, and then lifted her long pearly nightgown. Marla's pale skin gleamed in the light, so silky, so white, so totally naked.

"Baby doll," he said softly, sounding pleasantly surprised, "you didn't wear any panties tonight. You really *are* a bad girl."

That made her blush, something rare for Marla, and she turned her head away. Zachary said her name again, in that low, cajoling way of his and she immediately looked back at him. His hands were warm on her body. He touched her delicately, as easily as he plucked the strings on his guitar. Sometimes when they made love, she felt as if they were on stage, could hear the sound of applause in her head.

Connie lay in bed wearing her most-treasured old nightgown, one in which comfort won over attractiveness. With Ron out of town, she could wear whatever she wanted without listening to any of his critical comments about her "granny flannel." She had several pillows propped up behind her as she read Maurice Sendak's classic picture book *Where the Wild Things Are*. Turning the pages, she grinned, imagining how she'd use the book on the first day of school and how the children would react. Then she looked at the stuffed "Wild Thing" doll that occupied the pillow next to hers. "They'll love it," she said to the doll, "and they'll love you, too."

She was making a carefully printed note in her classroom planner when the phone on the bedside table rang. Without stressing her mental abilities in the slightest, she knew who was on the other end: Ron, calling from the East Coast. He touched base with her at the same time every evening when he was out of town, as regimented in his personal schedule as he was in the way he organized his clothes.

"Hi, sweetie," she said. "How's it going?"

As Ron filled her in about this conference and that sales meeting, Connie made a face at the doll, indicating that Ron's story was less than fascinating. At one point, she even put the receiver up to the doll's ear, and then silently joked, "He does go on, doesn't he?"

When Ron had concluded his story, he said, "Look, it's late here, Connie. I'll call tomorrow."

"Same time," Connie said, more to herself than to her husband, "same channel."

"What was that?"

"Nothing," Connie laughed. "I love you." She replaced the receiver, then began moving books off the bed. Finally, she picked up the doll, about to set it by the jumble of belongings on the crowded nightstand, but then she stopped. "Okay," she said. "If you insist, you can sleep with me this one time. But you have to promise to keep your mouth shut about it when Ron gets home."

She ran her fingers through the doll's crazy mass of orange yarn hair, then snapped off the light. In the dark, she said, "You know, he can be so jealous."

The Wild Thing said nothing, and Connie closed her eyes.

Ron attempted to untangle the ivory-colored phone cord from

around his nubile bedmate. "How'd you get so wrapped up in this?"

Deleen laughed. "You moved a lot while you were talking. Didn't seem to even notice that you were tying me up as you talked. Guilt got the best of you, I guess."

"But you're the one who's so well-bound—"

"Yeah," Deleen agreed, fluttering her lengthy ebony lashes at him. "What's that tell you?" She shot him a look that was definitely a dare, and he read her desires easily. That was one of the things he appreciated most about their connection. There was never any guessing involved. Deleen could tell him what she wanted simply by raising her eyebrows and turning her bee-stung lips upward in one of her devious smiles.

Deftly, Ron unhooked both ends of the curly cord from the hotel's phone. Rather than untie Deleen, he now worked to capture the brunette beauty even more securely with the cord. He liked the way she looked, naked except for the plastic phone wire, like a piece of modern art. "You're going to be completely in my power," he assured her. "You'll have to do anything I say. Anything at all."

"Yes, Master," she giggled happily. "But Ron?"

"Mm hmm," he mumbled, still working.

"With me so well-captured, and everything, it seems to me that *you're* the one who's going to have to do all of the dirty work." She tugged gently on the plastic bindings to prove her point.

"Not a problem," Ron said, moving easily between her lean thighs and licking gently toward the prize of her sex. "Because, really, I don't consider this work, at all." He switched back and forth at a slow pace, lapping along the inside of one leg, then switching over to the other, not leaving any part of her luscious body wanting for attention. Her skin felt like silk, tasted like perfume, and he marveled as he always did at how hungry she made him. Each motion forward further aroused his desire, but he took his time, because he knew that when he finally reached his goal, the rewards would be innumerable. "You like that, Del?" he asked, mouth pressed against her lustrous skin. "Like how that feels?"

Deleen, usually an extremely cooperative communicator, could only sigh in response.

"Cat got your tongue?" he asked next, moving slowly upwards. Nectar had spread to her inner thighs and as Ron licked her clean Deleen moaned softly. He rubbed his head back and forth, tickling her most sensitive region with his curly hair. This made her moan a bit louder, which was exactly what Ron was hoping for. He loved how vocal his girlfriend was. Connie never said a word when they did it, absolutely contained within her, which was how she'd always been from the very beginning. Unable to fully let loose. So different from his wife, Deleen seemed perfectly in tune with her needs. She believed that it was important to let him know what she wanted, and when she wanted it. Like now, as she captured him in a light scissor-hold between her legs and held him against her body, insisting with a forward thrust of her hips for him to continue his passionate licking games.

There was no problem at all with that. He was ready and more than willing. His tongue was rough, like an animal's, and just the feel of it against Deleen's body brought her close to a climax. He knew from experience that if he ran his tongue in the right manner up and down just a few more times, she would collapse, her body shaking with decadent spasm after spasm. When he glanced up, he saw that Deleen had shut her eyes tight, was obviously trying to keep herself still. He could tell from the tension in her body that she didn't want to give in too soon.

"You're so smooth—" he murmured, his fingers tracing over her nearly naked skin. Only "nearly" because she'd gone in for a new wax job: bare with a flair. This meant that while her entire sex was completely nude, a sparkling design of crystals adorned her exposed skin. The concept thrilled him. What a minx she was to go out and get a decoration that only an elite few would ever see. Again he thought of the differences between his lover and his wife. He couldn't imagine Connie ever doing anything to bring attention to the space between her legs. In fact, he couldn't picture her going into a salon and having the nerve to request any sort of wax job at all.

Now, Ron backed up a space and admired his lady, then moved in close again. He played connect the dots with his tongue as he moved from one crystal decoration to the next. His tongue flicked over those raised crystals then bestowed attention on the space between them. Finally, his open mouth circled her own hot little gem, lips pursed around it as if blowing her a kiss. Instinctively, he knew just how to touch her, nipping and biting on that most tender spot, circling it with his lips and suckling. He treated her pulsing jewel as if it were something precious, something breakable, using his tongue gently at first. Then he switched techniques and worked at a faster pace, his lips tightening, his very breath becoming an instrument of pleasure, blowing hot and hard against her.

Within seconds, he was making her moan and arch her body, murmuring his name, growing louder every moment—

The dream lover was waiting patiently, as before. Connie shivered.

"What are you afraid of, Connie? Having a good time?" He stood and moved toward her. She backed away. "No use running. There's no one to help you. Your husband's out of town tonight."

"How do you know about my husband?"

"I know what you know," he explained again. "Everything you know. Haven't you been paying attention?"

"I don't believe you."

"Take your randy redheaded friend. I know that she wouldn't resist me the way you do. She'd be spread out on the bed already, legs wide, panties in a puddle of black silk on the floor. In fact, she probably is in a similar position right now with that rough-and-ready musician boyfriend of hers. You just know that they're animals when they do it, don't you? Some people really know how to get down to business. She gives sex a good name."

"Marla?" Connie asked, knowing even as she said the name aloud that she sounded dense.

"Your college roommate. Your best friend. She even asked you to forward me to her when you described our meeting at lunch today. Good choice on the wine, by the way. I always go for a Chardonnay during the day. After dark, I generally choose Johnny Walker Red." Connie stared at him, fascinated, as if unable to look away. "But I don't want to be with her," the man continued in his easy-going manner. "I don't do sluts. I want you."

Connie stammered, unsure of what to say. "She's not a—"

"You still don't believe me, do you, kid? That's okay. I can prove myself, if I have to. Should I recite your social security number?"

"No."

"Your American Express card number?"

Connie shook her head.

"Your skirt size? Your bra size? You've got such pretty breasts, Connie. Why do you wear those plain cotton bras? Haven't you ever been to Victoria's Secret?" He put his hands to his temples, as if performing a hokey mind-reading act. "Yes, you have. I can see it now very clearly, as if I was in the pink-papered dressing room with you while you tried on lacy confections with your buddy. Now, there's a wet dream come to life. You and Marla stripping down to your little undies and choosing fantasy wear." He gave a low chuckle before continuing. "Yes, I can see that you've been there on several occasions. Each time you were accompanying Marla before one of her big dates. But you've never bought anything for yourself because you're too embarrassed to place those frilly confections on the counter. Besides that, what would Ron think? He doesn't really appreciate change, does he? What would he say if he found you in a lipstick-red lace thong rather than your normal good-girl white Jockey bikinis—"

"Stop!"

"So with all the things I know, of course I'm fully aware that your husband flew to Washington this morning. And, of course, I know that he had dinner this evening at Clyde's." He shrugged, indicating how trivial this all was for him. "I know that he's traveling in order to sell more franchises for his ridiculous bicycle messenger service."

Connie started to say something, but stopped. The man replied as if answering her unspoken comment.

"Yes, it *is* ridiculous. Even if it made him two million dollars last year. Men shouldn't wear Lycra biking shorts. They look like girls."

"You're reading my mind."

"What did you think? That I'm a magician? This isn't a parlor game, Connie. I'm most definitely reading your mind, and I read that you are more than due for some pleasure with your dream lover." He snapped his fingers and Crazy Town's hit song "Butterfly" began playing. The lyrics were deeply sexual, and the entrancing beat found its way beneath Connie's skin.

Since its release, Connie had liked both the song and the video that accompanied it, despite the fact that she felt she was about ten years older than MTV's intended demographic. This was one of her secret fancies. She'd never admitted to anyone that she thought the boys in the band, with their wild antics and colorful tattoos were completely sexy. She hadn't even told Marla, who had no problem confessing that she would sleep with the nineteen-year-old lead actor on the hit series *Dawson's Creek* if given a chance. Marla was an equal opportunity lover, with no prejudice against youth.

"I know you better than you know yourself. You like the idea of spending time with me, despite what you told your buddy over that mind-blowing chocolate brownie today. Admit it, Connie. The concept of having a mental affair turns you on. No strings. No worries. No ties. That is, except those ties that you fantasize about. A pair of cool metal handcuffs sometimes, when you want to push the boundaries. Or white silken bindings holding your wrists firmly above your head while I take care of your—"

"Stop—" Connie said again, but this time she spoke less emphatically.

The man stepped closer. As he moved, his jeans and oxford shirt were seamlessly transformed into a neat black tuxedo. In one hand, he held out a bouquet of violets, as if a peace offering. He took another step in her direction. With each motion forward he took on an image of someone or something that Connie found erotic. An officer in a crisply pressed white uniform. A rock star in form-fitting black leather pants and tight crimson shirt. A road worker sporting bulging muscles. A seductive golf pro she'd taken lessons from once on vacation—until finally he had reached her side and was back in jeans and plain shirt. Connie sensed the changes within her as they took place, and she blinked her eyes quickly, trying to keep the man in clear focus.

"Connie, when you understand the possibilities, you'll realize how wonderful this is. Most women would kill to find themselves in this sort of situation. Without your asking, I'll make all of your forbidden fantasies come true." For a moment, the lights in the room flickered, and when they came up again, the room had become a beach, hot sand on the ground at their bare feet, the sound of the ocean all around them. It was the image Connie had touched herself to in the bath before Ron's trip. The man had on a pair of turquoise-and-white surf shorts, revealing a washboard-flat stomach and well-muscled legs. Connie's own drab nightgown had morphed into a sleek black bikini. She looked stunning in the get-up, but she immediately put one hand to her face, hiding, and the other hand across her body, covering her near nakedness. Connie could smell the scent of the surf, and the perfumed fragrance of tropical suntan lotion.

The man raised his arms up as if conducting an invisible symphony and the room changed again, this time with the lights still on, finding yet another one of Connie's all-time favorite fantasies. With a sudden motion that Connie felt deep in her stomach, the two were on a moving Ferris wheel, one that Connie had ridden in Paris years before on a trip she'd taken after college graduation. Oh, how she'd loved Paris. From this height, Connie could see all of city spread panoramically around her, the beautiful old buildings and well-manicured parks and gardens.

The man had his hand high up on her thigh, and he squeezed her gently, then worked his fingers down to the hem and began to slide his hand up under the fabric of her skirt. She looked down to see that she was no longer wearing a bikini, but was now dressed in a chic short white suede skirt and a black silk turtleneck. She had on high-heeled leather boots, a style she'd always admired but never given in to. Silver zippers ran up the sides of her calves and the boots ended in dramatic spiked heels.

Connie gazed over the edge of the Ferris wheel car, looking at the carnival far below. She remembered that when she'd been on the ride, she'd thought it would be the sexiest place to make out, if not to actually make love. She closed her eyes as the man kissed her, feeling his warmth, knowing that somehow this was actually happening. This was a dream come true.

The sunlight caressed her skin. The sounds of traffic lifted up to her from the busy intersection below. They were near the Louvre Museum, near the arcade of the ritzy Rue de Rivoli—they were in France. The fantasy felt so real that Connie knew she couldn't resist much longer. Giving in would equal such intense bliss. And why was she holding out anyway? Who would it hurt if she let her fantasies take over?

"Beauty," the man said, sensing her desire to give in. His fingers traced along the rise of her cheekbones, then continued upward, getting lost in her hair. "I love your mind. There are so many ways, so many possibilities—"

He kissed her again, as the Ferris wheel started to move. As the machinery whirred into motion, Connie let herself kiss him back. Her entire body felt alive with the amazing sensations of giving in. She felt as if she were flying as their car traveled up even higher, then started the long crest down. The man moved his hands to her shoulders, then wandered them down the front of her sweater, cupping her breasts. She sat up straighter, offering herself to him, feeling a tremulous pleasure work through her.

When she opened her eyes, the scene changed again, and this time the two were in the back seat of a vintage Mustang, the kind her boyfriend had owned in high school. She smelled the leather interior, felt the man's hands still on her, moving slowly under her pastel blue cashmere sweater to touch her naked skin, and suddenly she'd had enough of the wizardry. There were too many ideas to process, too much to take in too fast.

Opening the car door, Connie turned and ran, finding herself at a deserted drive-in movie theater. She heard no sound of pursuit, but when she turned around, she saw the man's image up there on the movie screen, larger than life. He was straddling a fancy motorcycle, leaning forward on the handlebars like some icon from the fifties.

As she stared up at him, he called after her, "So you want to play hide-and-seek? That's fine with me, baby. I have all the time you need. But I ought to warn you, Connie, I'm very good at that game. You can hide yourself anywhere you want. I'll always find you." He revved the engine of the Harley, and above the sound of the roaring motor, he said, "Go hide while I count to fifty. One, two, three—"

"Explain it again," Zach insisted, gazing up Marla's naked body in awe. They had already made love one time. Now, they were gearing up for their second round, and Marla had something new she wanted to try. As she explained her desires to Zach, he leaned forward with one hand outstretched, but Marla wasn't ready. And if she wasn't ready, that meant that Zach had to wait for her to give him the green light.

"No, don't touch me." She shook her head back and forth deliberately, and a sexy smile danced in her comely blue eyes. "I want you to hold off until you can guess exactly what I want."

"Guess?"

"Read my mind—"

"That's what this is all about? The psychic mumbo-jumbo you said Connie talked about at lunch?"

"Connie's whole story just turned me on so much. Some imaginary guy appeared to her who could intuit every fantasy she'd ever had. And make all of her fantasies come true. What could be more of a turn-on than that?"

"Come on, Marla," Zach sighed, laying back on the mattress. "Even if it really did happen the way Connie said, what sort of fantasies could she possibly have in that uptight head of hers?

She's a schoolteacher, for God's sake. She wears penny loafers—with actual shiny copper pennies in them. I've never met anyone more pure than she is. She probably fantasizes about doing it missionary-style in the dark."

Marla pursed her lips and looked at him. Extremely protective of Connie, she didn't like anyone saying anything negative about her best friend. Regardless of the fact that what Zachary said was true.

"Remember what she was like at your New Year's party?" Zach continued. "All the guests were making out madly at midnight, losing themselves in the moment, and when I glanced over at Connie she was standing there by herself looking miserable.

"The key words there are 'by herself.' Ron should have been kissing her to ring in the New Year, not off in some corner most likely flirting with someone else. What an ass. He didn't want to come in the first place and was pulling on her the whole time to leave. And besides," Marla continued emphatically, "you never know what's going on in someone's head. It's the repressed ones who are really wild in their minds. Don't you read the papers? You have no idea what Connie thinks about in bed. She's probably even kinkier than you are."

Zach looked back at Marla. "But why are we playing this game? *You're* not repressed. Just think of the things we've done together."

"I know," she grinned. "You've got it easy, baby. You simply have to choose something on the menu and see if it's what I'm thinking about tonight."

Tilting his head to one side, Zach said, "All right, sweetheart. I'm going to choose one item from the appetizer list, another for my main course, and for the finale, you'll be dessert."

"Mmm," Marla sighed. "I do like the sound of that."

Shaking herself awake, Connie jumped out of bed and quickly, carelessly, got dressed. It was as if she were still dreaming, still escaping from the dream lover. Her feet moved without the help of her mind, hurrying her down the stairs and into the kitchen. For a moment, she hesitated in front of the cream-colored Princess phone mounted on the wall.

Call Ron? He'd make fun of her, maybe, but she could pretend she'd forgotten to give him an important phone message. Simply hearing his calm, rational voice would make her feel better. She knew it. Frantically, she fumbled with papers on the refrigerator, searching for his hotel information. When she finally found the phone number, she dialed and requested his room without giving herself time to talk herself out of it. After several rings, the lilting voice of the hotel operator came back on the line.

"No answer, Miss. Would you like to leave a message?"

He was undoubtedly at the hotel gym working out, his general routine when on the road. He would pound his way along the fast-moving rubber track of the treadmill, then pump iron for an hour. He'd always needed less sleep than she did. No, Connie wouldn't leave a message. What could she say? "Call your over-reacting wife—she had a nightmare and can't fall asleep." Instead, she hung up and looked around the empty kitchen. On the table in the center of the cherry-red Formica, sat a fresh arrangement of violets. The scent fueled her need for escape.

Without thinking about the insanity of what she was doing, she grabbed her car keys and purse, rushed out through the front door, and got into her car. Beneath the light of the full moon, Connie drove down the darkened street. Once she was away from the house, and at the end of the road, she stopped the car and just waited. Her breathing was rapid, and the sound filled the air around her. This was nuts. Leaving her house because of a dream pursuer? It didn't make any sense.

Exhausted, she crossed her arms over the steering wheel, set her head down, and closed her eyes. Immediately, she could hear the man counting, his voice so loud that it felt as if he were sitting in the back seat of the car. Starting violently, she glanced over her shoulder at the empty seat, then tried to shake the cobwebs of the dream from her mind. With no thoughts of where she was going, she pulled the car away from the curb and began driving erratically around the block. Stopped at a red light around the corner from her house, she looked up and saw a billboard featuring a sultry redhead at a computer monitor. The model looked like her best friend.

"Marla," Connie said, gunning the engine.

She and Marla had been best friends for nearly ten years, since they'd wound up roommates together in one of UCLA's freshmen dorms. Although they couldn't have been more different, their friendship was the strongest bond she'd ever experienced with anyone—including her husband. Marla had been her maid of honor, her closest confidant, the one person who always knew how to calm her down in any sort of crisis. Without a doubt, she would be willing to help.

Connie felt better as she drove the few miles to Marla's apartment. But when she pulled into Marla's parking lot, she slowed and saw a chili-red Harley parked in Marla's spot. The license plate on the motorcycle read "ZAX," and Connie looked up into the window at Marla's apartment and saw the wavy golden light of candles behind the transparent curtain. Sighing, she pulled out and started to drive again.

No, Marla probably wouldn't mind being disturbed, but Connie was far too polite to go knocking, and too embarrassed to have a half-naked Zachary greet her at the door. At the next intersection, Connie closed her eyes again. "I'll always find you," the dream lover murmured in her head. His voice jolted Connie into consciousness as quickly as if she'd been doused with water, and with great effort she drove on, like an athlete coaxing herself to the finish line of a great race.

Driving past her favorite 24-hour bakery, she nodded to herself, pulled a quick U-turn and parked the car in the nearly empty lot. Coffee and donuts. No, just coffee. That's what she needed. Before she got out of the car, Connie checked her reflection in the rearview mirror. She looked like hell, confused and slightly crazed in a plaid shirt of Ron's and an old pair of jeans. She'd had no sleep in two days, and it showed. She was wearing zero makeup, and her hair couldn't have been more of a mess. But so what? People who went out for donuts at two in the morning weren't supposed to be all neat and pressed.

Opening the door, she lurched from the car and stumbled into the restaurant. Bright fluorescent lights buzzed overhead and one lone male customer sat hunched over in a corner booth working on a laptop.

"Coffee, please," she said to the multiply pierced college-age kid behind the counter.

"Decaf or regular?"

"Regular. Extra-regular. Regular with a shot of espresso, actually."

"Some donuts to go with that?"

Connie eyed the sugar-filled display. "No."

The clerk could tell from her expression that she was tempted, and just as the waiter had earlier in the day, he played on her obvious weakness. "They're fresh—"

Connie shook her head.

"They're yummy—"

He pulled a large, chocolate-glazed donut from the display and held it out to Connie. When she put her hand up in protest, the boy took a large bite himself, then went to make her coffee at the old-fashioned silver espresso machine on the rear counter. Connie set her hands on the cool glass display case and put her head down as she waited. Sleep claimed her instantly. In her head, she could hear the dream lover talking to her, crooning with a seductive voice like a blues singer. Too many people were trying to get her to do something. The clerk wanted her to eat donuts. The man wanted her to give in.

"I'll take one," she said to the young man when he returned with her coffee.

"One what?" he asked, messing with her. The silver hoops in his ears shined in the bright lights.

"A donut, okay?"

She took her coffee and treat and left without putting a tip in the jar which was an odd move for Connie. Back in the car, she turned the air conditioning on to the highest setting and rolled down the windows. Fresh, cold air would keep her awake—that and the jumbo-sized cup of pure caffeine in her cup holder. As she drove, she took a scalding sip of the coffee, spilling some in her haste.

"Oh, shoot—" Connie muttered, her vocabulary G-rated even when students weren't present. She pulled to the side of the road and wiped at her damp shirt. And then, because she'd gone for too long without sleep, she put her head down again. In her mind, she could see the dream lover on the bed, smiling. He had on a pair of black Wayfarer sunglasses, which he dipped low as he looked at her appreciatively.

"Hey, baby," he whispered to her. "I found you. Didn't I tell you I was good at this game? You can't win, Connie. So why not give in? Think how good it will feel."

Waking with a start, Connie stared out the windshield. She reached into her purse and pulled out her cell phone, but as she pushed the digits to dial Marla's number, the battery icon flashed.

No juice. With the hectic pace of the impending start of the school year, she'd forgotten to charge the thing. Ron generally took care of that sort of stuff for her, always into his orderly systems.

What to do?

Down the block stood an old-fashioned telephone booth, like an antique remnant from another era. She drove to it, parked the car again, and walked into the glass-encased area. From memory, Connie dialed Marla's number. She knew that it would be okay to interrupt even the best sex in an emergency.

But Marla was screening. "I can't come to the phone now," her friend's taped voice purred over the wire. "Maybe I'm out having fun." Low provocative laugh. "Or maybe I'm *in* having fun. To find out, leave your name and number and I'll call you back when I come up for air—" Connie hesitated for a moment—but what could she say that wouldn't sound nuts?—and then resignedly, she hung up.

"Who's calling you this late?" Zachary wanted to know.

Marla, mouth busy at the center of his body, didn't respond.

Zachary wanted an answer, and he wrapped his hands in her cherry-colored curls and tilted her head so that she was looking up his body and toward his face. His expression was both stern and concerned. "Come clean, baby," he said.

"Sales call?" Marla murmured, letting his erection slip free from her hungry lips.

"After midnight? What could they possibly be selling?"

"You jealous, Zach?" she asked the question with a wink, to soften the statement, and the tease in her voice simply added to the hot pulse of electricity between them.

"I just like to understand what I'm dealing with. All the players in the situation, you know? Phone calls in the wee hours generally have less to do with business and more to do with pleasure. Is there someone else who should be joining us?"

"Ah, I get what you're saying," Marla grinned. "But that's just your incredibly filthy mind at work. The phone rings and you immediately think 'orgy.'" As she spoke, Marla climbed onto his body, straddling him at the waist. Zachary had an irresistible physique. He was lean, with corded muscles, and the pale parts of his skin seemed simply like empty canvas, waiting for a tattoo artist's pen. Looking down at her lover, Marla traced her fingertips over the rise of his high-cut cheekbones, then moved her fingers down to rest on his full lips. His tongue flicked out to touch her fingers, and she shivered all over at the delicious sensation. The warmth of such a wet caress fueled her passion. "There's only one player here that you need to worry about."

Zachary gripped tightly into her waist and slid her body up and down his steel-like erection, sweetly wet from the ministrations of her knowledgeable mouth. He moved her once, twice, and then held her in place, body pressed to body, so that she was sealed perfectly to him. Zach knew how to treat her. He ran his fingertips along the insides of her thighs, and she trembled at his touch, squeezing hard on him. This was exactly what Zachary was hoping for, and he kept up the soft massage. His fingers made circles, then diamonds, and he worked them closer and closer to the split between her legs. Then he rocked his hips upward, bouncing Marla on his rod, and she ground her body against his and sighed.

Now that he was actually captured within her, Marla found it difficult to think. Yet she always liked to talk during sex. To see how far she could keep up a conversation. It was a fun game to play. Even when she failed to make any sounds other than moans, there were never any losers.

"I'm all yours," she told him. "That is, if you can handle me."

Her mind went cloudy again as Zach's hands wandered upward to caress her breasts. His strong fingers found her tender nipples and pinched them gently at first and then less gently.

"Don't worry about that, baby," Zachary grinned at her. "I can handle anything you have to offer."

Back in her car, Connie headed south on Highway 101 toward Los Angeles. There was no reason for this choice of direction. She could just as easily have gone north, traveling across the majestic Golden Gate Bridge and toward the peaceful regions of Marin. With Marla too busy to answer her call, or too sound asleep in post-coital bliss to hear it, Connie had no one else to turn to, nowhere else to go.

A light rain began to fall, and Connie closed the windows and turned on the windshield wipers, then flicked on the radio. As if to taunt her further, the raucous beat of Crazy Town's hit single poured immediately from the speakers. Angrily, she shut off the music. Looking out of the wet glass of the windshield, her vision blurred. Raindrops formed liquid crystals in front of her eyes, and she blinked hard as her car started to drift from lane three into the fast lane. A tanker truck nearly plowed into her Volvo. The trucker blasted his horn fiercely as he sped by. Tears slid rapidly down Connie's cheeks as she drove onto a frontage road and pulled into the parking lot of the Creekside Motel. It was raining harder now, and Connie sat frozen in the front seat, unable to make herself move.

"It's all a dream," she told herself. "I'm home in bed fast asleep. This isn't happening to me." Her voice grew hoarse as she tried to calm herself. "When the alarm blasts, I'll hit the snooze button, skip the shower today, and sleep some more."

A motel clerk, who had spotted her through the large plate glass window, rushed outside with a large black umbrella and helped Connie indoors. "This way, Miss. Just a few steps and you'll be warm and dry."

"I need a room," she said. Giant tears streaked over her cheeks, and her stained clothes were buttoned incorrectly. The clerk sympathetically helped her fill out a registration form, taking the information he needed and printing it in the boxes on the photocopied sheet. It was obvious that he'd seen worse cases than Connie's and he made no comment about her lack of luggage or abrupt arrival. After only a moment of bureaucratic workings, he located a key, and then led Connie to her room.

Once inside Room 117, she stood against the cheaply painted apple green wall for a moment, trying to get her bearings. What was she doing here? Nothing made sense to her. She looked around the depressing room for several seconds before going into the tiny bathroom, with its dingy mirror and cracked tiles. There was even a white strip of paper wrapper over the toilet to show that it had been sanitized "for her protection."

In this minuscule space, she splashed her face with several handfuls of icy cold water. The person looking back at her from the mirror didn't resemble her mental image of herself in the slightest. The woman she saw was wild-eyed with windswept hair and tear-stained features. How had she gotten to this point so quickly? She was only forty-five minutes from her home, but she felt as if the distance were thousands of miles.

Sadly, she returned to the main room, sat on the sagging mattress, turned on the TV, and channel surfed. After bits of an old movie, a news show, and a religious broadcast, Connie stopped at a noisy tractor pull contest. As she sat upright in bed facing the television, her eyes finally closed.

"Talk to me, Marla," Zachary crooned, his full lips pressed right against Marla's ear. "Tell me what you want."

"You know what I want," she said, trying not to laugh. It was difficult to stay serious. Especially now that Zachary had her held firmly to the bed with several ruby red silken ties she kept in the top drawer of her bedside table for just this type of passionate purpose. That drawer was filled with Marla's array of sexual supplies — edible cherry-flavored lubricant, clips and clamps of different sizes and strengths, feathers, potions that grew hot when breathed upon, vibrators and dildos in a rainbow of colors. But Zachary wanted only the ties this evening, prepared to do all of the rest of the work himself.

Marla's slim wrists were bound over her head. Her ankles were attached to the bedposts, legs spread wide apart.

"Spell it out for me," he insisted. "Pretend that I'm slow."

"You are slow," she sighed. "So slow. And, man oh man, that is such a good thing right now."

"Then tell me whether I'm getting warmer," he said, resuming those bewitching tricks with the tip of his tongue, heading directly to the location that most needed his attention. Slowly, his mouth moved up her body. He took his time, licking and kissing, making Marla shiver all over at his masterful touch. She stared upward, at the top of her canopied bed, the layer of sheer pearly fabric that draped like a translucent cloud over her head.

"Warmer—" Marla whispered. "Oh, warmer."

As he traveled up her inner thighs at his wickedly slow pace, Marla groaned and arched her hips skyward, talking with her body rather than her words. Zachary had a magic mouth. When he took his time, he could bring Marla to the edge of climax again and again, teasing her back down and then refueling her internal fires.

"I want to hear you say it," Zachary insisted. "Tell me what you want—"

And Marla closed her eyes, and parted her lips, and gave in. "I want you—" she sighed. "Oh, do I want you."

"Say it," he demanded. "Let me know exactly how to please you."

"I want you to use your tongue," she continued, growing more impatient by the second.

"Where?"

She would have pointed if she could have, but with her wrists over her head, all she could do was continue to strain upwards. "You know."

"Tell me," he urged, his mouth poised.

"Please—" she begged, and he moved into place and began to dine.

# CHAPTER FOUR

The whiskey-edged voice of Keith Richards sang softly, filling the room with the sound and mood of a blues club. The song was "Thief in the Night," a Rolling Stones' number that Connie adored, and now the music played in the background while her dream lover waited for her on the bed. When Connie turned to look for speakers, she saw a vintage jukebox standing in the corner, complete with iridescent blue and orange neon lights that flickered up and down to the beat as the music played. Every time she visited this strange mental region, the room became more complete, more perfectly in tune with her personal style.

Now, drawn toward the sound of one of her most beloved bands, she began to flip through the range of audio selections. Each song displayed was one of her all-time favorites: "Dream On" by Aerosmith. "Every Breath You Take" by the Police. "One" by U2. Led Zeppelin's "D'yer Mak'er." Lou Reed's "Wild Side." Mixed in with the classic rock tunes were oddball selections that she'd never told anybody she liked—oldies from the fifties like "Little Red Riding Hood" by Sam Sham and the Pharaohs mingled with several punk selections from the seventies and ska classics like UB40's "Red, Red Wine." Eclectic and unusual, these were the tunes that most pleased Connie, and each one was there, staring at her.

How did he know?

As soon as the question formed in her mind, she realized the answer. It was time for her to accept that the man knew everything. Like the fact that she most adored making love in the romantic ambiance of candlelight, something that Ron rarely had time for anymore.

"Save the candles for emergencies," he'd said the last time Connie had attempted to light a small vanilla-scented candle by their bed. "Just turn the light out like normal people."

Yet here, in this fantasy place, several twisted ivory candles burned on a low table, dancing dramatic shadows across the wall. The man did know her well, didn't he? Everything about this place was geared to her pleasure—the music, the lighting, the warmth of the room. So why should she continue to fight him? Looking confused and slightly defeated, Connie moved toward the bed—and toward the waiting lover.

"Did I find you, or did you find me?" the dream lover asked in a sexy voice, taking her hand and drawing her into bed.

"I'm so tired."

"Tired of what, Connie?"

She contemplated her answer before speaking, then slowly said, "Tired of running away."

"Now's the time to stop running. I'm right here, waiting for you. I've been here all along. You're the one putting off the inevitable." He hesitated. "And that's not all you're tired of, is it?"

Of course, it wasn't. And, of course, he would be able to see in her mind what she'd refused to say out loud. She was tired of being taken for granted. All Ron did was use her, expect her to be ready for him when he was in the mood, without ever considering her own needs. Had she really fallen for so selfish a lover? Had he always been that way, or had something important changed between them—a subtle shift that happened so slowly she hadn't noticed?

Before she could find the answers to these questions, the dream lover took charge. He kissed her cheek and then, taking her face between his hands, kissed her lips. Firmly, he stroked her arms and her back. Even in this dreamy place, she was drenched from the rain, and he undressed her carefully, as if unwrapping a present. Her mismatched clothes soon lay in a damp heap at her feet, and she stood naked and beautiful in the circle of light with her pale lustrous skin, soft curves, and her long hair wet and gently curling over her shoulders.

She heard a crackling sound and realized as she looked around that a fire had appeared behind her in an old-fashioned stone fireplace. The heat spread through her body with delicious ease, removing the chill from the rain.

"I still don't know who you are—"

"That doesn't matter. Nothing matters except how you feel. And, Connie?"

He waited until he was certain that she was focused on each word. "I'll make you feel so good."

"I need to see your face. I need to know," she shrugged, hoping that he'd understand how important this was for her. "That's just how I am."

"Is that all you need, Connie?"

She nodded. Suddenly, the shadows shifted, and she was looking at Marla's handsome boyfriend Zachary, a man she'd always thought stunning, although she'd never fully admitted this to herself. How could she fess up to the fact that she thought her best friend's man was attractive? Desirable, even. Yet as she stared at the Zachary replica, she knew something was amiss. Sure, he looked exactly like Zach, from his long dark hair to the tattoos on his muscular arms, but the voice was wrong, didn't match Zach's southern drawl, his slow and easy way of talking.

"Now you see?"

"But you're not Zach."

As quickly as his features had been revealed, the dream lover's face transformed into the visage of the chiseled male model decorating the cover of Connie's current favorite romance novel—dark hair, dimpled chin, striking green eyes. She squinted her eyes at him, as he shape-shifted once again to the movie star who always managed to make her come in her fantasies. The one she thought about sometimes when she and Ron slept together and she couldn't even get close to the finish line without added mental assistance.

"I don't understand."

"I can be anyone you want," the man whispered to her. "I can do anything you need—anything you've ever dreamed of. You're beautiful, Connie. Let me. Just *let* me."

"But who are you? What do I call you?"

"Does it really matter?"

Maybe it didn't. Maybe she could just go with it. Maybe—

Sensing her indecision and her will to give in, the man acted immediately. In a blink, he was naked, holding her in his arms on the bed. The feel of his body against hers made Connie sigh and close her eyes.

Yes, she could give in. Because it felt too good not to.

"Don't worry so much, Connie," the man instructed. "Just relax."

They began to make love with gentle ease. There was no rushing. No previously choreographed patterns to follow. It had been years since she'd been with a man aside from Ron. Years since she felt that flutter of anticipation in the base of her stomach, letting her know that something amazing was going to happen.

The man's hands roamed over Connie's body. He touched her arms, ran his fingers along the ridge of her shoulder blades, then tickled them down her spine. In spite of herself, she groaned softly with pleasure. Shivers of pure bliss flooded through Connie and she trembled all over. Knowingly, the man brought his lips against her throat and kissed her.

"Pretty baby," her dream lover crooned softly, "my little girl likes that, doesn't she?"

Yes, Connie liked it. She liked everything he was doing. But before she could answer verbally, the man licked in one long line down the hollow of her throat. Warmth washed over her. He lingered against her pulse point as if feeling her heartbeat, before biting the fine chain of her gold necklace, tugging on it between his teeth.

*Oh, yes*, Connie thought. *That's it. That's right.* She didn't say the words out loud, but she knew that she didn't need to.

Slowly, he continued on his exploratory trip, moving lower, kissing along her fair skin until he reached her breasts. Now, he took one rose-colored nipple in her mouth, then the other, moving back and forth between them, getting them wet and slippery before teasing them with his teeth.

"Look how erect your nipples get," the man sighed. "Just the slightest touch has them hard as tiny stones."

Connie didn't have to look. She could tell from the sensations going on inside her exactly how hard her nipples were. Ron didn't have the time or the inclination to play like this anymore. After all of their years together, their occasional lovemaking had become one well-rehearsed event. Step one, followed by step two, followed by step three. She tried to remember the last time Ron had said that she was pretty, the last time he had watched her body for her responses, noticing what it took to turn her on. *This* man understood, focusing on areas usually ignored in Ron's rush to reach the climax and go take a shower, and his attentiveness made Connie more excited than she had been in years.

"It's just too bad," the man said, latching onto her thoughts. "Too bad that someone would waste an evening with you."

The dream lover worked steadily, taking her on an erotic ride through each stage of arousal. While softly caressing her left nipple with his lips and tongue, he used his hand on the other, pinching it between thumb and fingers until she moaned and turned her head away. Her mane of softly spun hair fell over her face, shielding her from what she could only guess was his fixed gaze.

"That's just what you need, isn't it?" The man crooned, moving his lips away for a second to talk to me. "Exactly what you want."

Yes, it was. The combination of a tiny spark of pain from his fingers mingled deliciously with the intense pleasure from his mouth. As he played her, the music changed once again. Now, a selection from the Red Hot Chili Peppers flowed forth, the lead-singer Anthony singing about liking pleasure spiked with pain.

It seemed that so did Connie. In a startling realization, she found that she wanted the man to pinch her nipples harder, to bite them. She wanted to truly feel it deep within herself.

*Make this real*, she thought. *Make me know that it's not just a dream.*

Still, she didn't say anything. She couldn't really believe these thoughts were filling her mind. She'd only experienced sweet sex in the past. Never rough. Never raw. These new sensations had her dripping, and she shifted her hips on the white cotton sheet, feeling the puddle of liquid sex forming beneath her. By the time the man made it down there, she would be positively soaking. But even though she was almost desperate, Connie didn't ask him to taste her, to lick her, to tease her between her thighs the way he was playing with her breasts. She sensed that he was working at his own pace, taking his time until she felt as if she might faint out of unquenched desire if he wouldn't let her come. When she told him this, the man simply laughed.

"You won't," he whispered, "you'll swoon with pleasure instead."

Connie was almost there now, her body arching, balancing like one of the graceful surfers she sometimes watched out at Santa Cruz beach riding the crest of an azure-blue wave. She lingered on the edge of climax for such a long time that she felt only a puff of air against her would make her come. Just a breath from the man's parted lips. She didn't even need his tongue on her, his fingers, his sex. Only a breath.

He didn't give it to her.

Instead, he moved now to straddle her body high up, and then he held her hands over her head. She was stretched out in this position, and her body shuddered with silent tremors as he looked down at her, holding her gaze. She could see his face clearly now. He wasn't Zach. He wasn't the model from the book cover. But although she didn't know his name, she recognized him. Here was the fantasy man she'd dreamed of for years with strong cheekbones, dark glossy hair, and eyes as deep and cobalt as blue velvet.

*Focus*, he seemed to be saying. *Pay attention to how you're feeling.*

Connie couldn't guess what his plan was, but she was fascinated by the sensation of being captured in his embrace. If he moved a little closer, she could flick her tongue out to touch him. She wanted his smell on her, his scent around her, wanted to swim in an ocean of pure sex.

He stayed back, teasing her with the distance. Making her whimper with yearning. She could only just barely catch her breath. She knew her cheeks were pink with embarrassment, but she felt fantastic anyway, as if she'd just run a marathon.

"You like that," he said. "The power of anticipation." It wasn't a question. He released her wrists, moved down slightly, and entered her. The impact was intense, and Connie gasped. He plunged forward once, pressing his body against hers. Everything she'd ever fantasized about seemed concentrated into this one moment of their two bodies connecting.

"You don't know if you're coming or going," The man continued, his smile broadening. He cocked his head at her. "*Now*, do you want me to stop?" he asked.

"Don't—" Connie begged. "No, don't stop. Don't ever stop."

# BOOK TWO

*Shall I come, sweet love, to thee*
*When the evening beams are set?*
—William Shakespeare

# CHAPTER FIVE

In the distance, a series of brilliant fireworks burst against the endless backdrop of a midnight sky. Multicolored blooms dripped slowly across the velvety darkness, disappearing in a shimmering haze as they fell down to earth. The tremendous reverberations of the fireworks were so loud that they seemed to be amplified, adding to their extravagant appeal.

Connie and her dream lover stood in the open window of a luxurious hotel suite, watching the explosions from a distance. Entirely nude, Connie leaned across the sill, feeling the breath of cool night air against her. The man took his position behind her, his hands roaming over her naked skin. His touch sent swells of delight throughout her body, and Connie held herself steady, knowing instinctively that a greater pleasure awaited her.

She sensed that when she turned to face him, the room would shift and change, transforming into anything she could possibly imagine. The muted red-painted walls would melt away, becoming an opening in a tropical forest, or an empty back alley behind a San Francisco blues club, or a tram overlooking the snow-covered Alps. The man would search her head for a vision that he found enticing, and then he'd make that experience come true. For now, she wanted to witness the beauty of the artwork in the sky.

And she wanted to do so while they made love.

His hands firm on her waist, he steadied her, then slid the first inch of his erection between her taut thighs. Each time a rocket exploded in the air, her dream lover drove deeper into her. His passion echoed the elation she received from watching the fireworks. The lights in the sky seemed close enough to touch.

"Let go, Connie," he urged.

"What?" she murmured. "What do you mean?"

"You can be loud here. You can be as loud as you like—"

She knew that he was right. "Here" didn't really exist. "Here" there was nobody but him and her. Besides, if she wanted to truly lose herself in the fantasy, then the fireworks would cover her cries. No one would hear the sound of her throaty pleasure. No one would know.

As he pushed forward, she swallowed hard. Could she do it? For years, she'd envied the girls in high school known as "screamers," the ones who weren't held back by their inhibitions. People like Marla, who felt it was their right to be able to express themselves vocally if that's what turned them on. Occasionally, Marla liked to brag about the neighbors banging on her walls when she and her man lost themselves in a moment. But Connie was different. She'd always retreated deep inside herself during any lovemaking session, focused too much on what Ron would think to ever really be able to let go. By this point, it was too late. If she ever started upping the volume during a sexual encounter, Ron would want to know what had changed. Had she been watching porno movies? Hanging out with Marla and her wicked crowd for too long? Learning from another lover?

"Now," the man urged, sensing exactly how she was feeling. "Forget about Ron. Forget about everyone. Don't worry yourself by thinking too much. Come on, Connie. You can do it. Do it for me." A pause and then, in a more serious tone, "Do it for you."

His fingers found the treasure between her thighs and he stroked it. Touched it. Rapped his fingers in the perfect rhythm up and over that sweetly pulsing gem. Connie closed her eyes for a moment and saw an echo of the fireworks painted on her shut lids. As the dream sped up the pace, moving his body harder against hers, she parted her lips and cried out with the pleasure of it. The release felt like nothing she'd ever experienced before.


Zachary woke up ready for more. As usual during one of their many sexual marathons, they hadn't gotten much sleep. There were too many ways to play, too many activities that they needed to try. But dream deprivation didn't matter to either one of them. Dark under-eye circles were acceptable payment in exchange for the many orgasms they'd shared. "You can sleep as long as you want when you're dead" was one of Zachary's favorite mottoes.

"Little kitty's getting furry," Zachary said, warm fingers wandering down under the leopard-print sheets to find Marla's usually well-pruned patch of fur. It had been a long week, and she'd skipped her routine waxing appointment in favor of a much-needed nap. But it wasn't as if she'd grown a beard. She was just a little fuzzier between her thighs than normal.

"I guess the honeymoon's over," he continued, feigning sadness.

"You're pretty furry, too," she told him, reaching down to firmly twine her own fingers in his short dark curls. "Maybe you should consider a visit to Julie."

"And Julie is—?"

"My waxer. She does men, too, you know."

"Bet she does," Zachary smiled. "I'll bet she does *lots* of men."

"I'm serious," Marla told him. "Half her clients are male."

He pushed up on one arm to look at her, stunned by the thought. "They wax their pubic hair?"

Yes, Marla honestly knew that most of the men who went to Julie wanted their back hair removed, or their chests to be as smooth as a Versace boy toy model, but she took advantage of Zachary's naivete because he'd been teasing her. "Uh, huh," she told him, nodding animatedly to show how truthful she was. "Maybe you should try it."

"Hot wax down there? I don't think so."

"She uses cold wax, too," she continued, "and there are other methods of hair removal, you know."

"So what are the benefits?" he asked seriously, "aside from having a strange woman's hand in your crotch." Marla could feel his rod stirring right below where her fingers were still nestled in his hair. This conversation was definitely appealing to his kinky side.

"Well," she told him, "you know the feeling of making love to me right after a wax job when I'm totally bare...?"

"'The sphinx," he said, naming the wax job she'd had that completely removed all hair. *Every* strand. His eyes glazed slightly at the memory.

"It'll feel like that for you. Just bare, smooth skin against mine."

His hand searched out the split between her legs again, fingers finding the reddish fur, and he said, "Not so smooth right now, baby."

"So let's fix it." She pushed out from under the covers and padded naked down the hall. After a moment, Zachary followed her to the bathroom and leaned against the cool lip of the sink as he got out the supplies. While he watched, Marla slipped into the shower and turned on the water. "Come on," she urged him. "Soap up first, to get everything warm and wet. Then we'll shave—"

"We?" he asked joining his lady under the hot spray.

"Tit for tat," she told him, "I shave you, you shave me."

They spent a few glorious minutes lathering each other up all over, and then Marla got into the frisky fun by using her pink-hued, raspberry scented, girly-girl conditioner on his pubic hair. But before he could get too turned on by this most personal shampoo session, she killed the water. She could tell from the look on his face that he was still undecided about their little erotic adventure, so she dried off, handed over the razor, and spread herself out on the fluffy bath mat. Immediately, Zachary took charge, slapping a towel around his flat waist and working her up with the lather, fingers probing and gently pinching to hold her lips still. In just a short time she was bare again. And revved up. Her body throbbed deliciously from all the attention it had just received.

Now it was his turn. "Ready, baby?" she asked. He nodded bravely and took a stand feet apart, weight set. First, Marla used a small pair of silvery scissors to trim his fur. Dark curls rained down onto the floor. Then slowly, she spread the shaving cream all over his skin, and Zachary sighed at the sensation of icy menthol. He closed his eyes when she got near him with the blade, but Marla had steady hands, and she whisked away all those short, black curls. As she rinsed him down with a soft cloth, she made sure that he could feel her hot breath on his skin. Then she parted her lips.

"What—" he murmured. "What are you doing?"

He'd thought they would immediately do it. She understood that he'd envisioned bending her over and taking her doggy-style against the sink. This was a favorite position of both Zachary and Marla because they could stare into the mirror on the back of the medicine cabinet, watching their reflections. But first, she wanted to reward him for being such a good sport. And, honestly, the way his sex looked without any hair framing it was a total and unexpected, turn-on. Just this majestic tower, waiting to feel her warm, wet lips around it.

She put her palms on his sturdy, muscled thighs as she brought her lips to the tip of his hard-on. Zachary sighed and traced his fingertips through her long curly hair as she drew the next inch of his shaft further into her mouth. There was something so unique about this experience and she had to use one hand to touch herself between her legs as she worked him. It was as if they were the most naked they'd ever been together.

Shorn. Bare. Smooth.

Sucking all the way down, she did her best to press her lips to the skin of his body, but he was just too long for this trick. Still, she got the contact she craved, running her fingertips along the silk-like skin of his body.

"Angel," Zachary whispered. "Don't stop."

She didn't. She kept sucking and swallowing, moving back on her heels to give herself room to simply lick his shaft. Her tongue in a point, she danced it up and down, caressing him, taunting him, until he just couldn't handle it any longer. He had to grab her shoulders, to bring her up to standing position, to take her against the sink.

As he met her reflection in the mirror, he murmured, "I think Julie's lost herself a customer—"

While Marla was lost in the real-life adventures of sex with a musician, Connie competed mentally on her own. Released from her daily, uptight surroundings, she swung her body around a silvery steel pole in the center of a deserted stage. Vibrant multicolored lights flashed on and off, illuminating the electric tiles below her feet in dizzying patterns. She looked down to see that she was wearing a pair of white vinyl high-heeled boots with clear synthetic heels. When she glanced in a full-length mirror across the way from the stage, she saw with a jolt of surprise that all she had on besides the boots was a scarlet-fringed bra and matching panties. Each time she moved her hips, the fringe danced with her, tickling her skin.

The music playing was a thunderous, hard-hitting song by Nine Inch Nails. Connie felt the beat as if it was throbbing within her body, and she danced. Oh, did she dance. Eyes focused on her reflection in the mirror she swished her hips in the most seductive way, moving sensually, snake-like.

The music continued, and Connie held the pole between her legs and slid down to a crouch. The metal was cool against her warm skin and she found that she liked the icy sensation. As she moved, the music changed, Nine Inch Nails giving way to Led Zeppelin's hit song "Black Dog."

Hadn't her dream lover confessed early on that he was a Zeppelin man? Was he choosing the selections now, playing deejay to her fantasies, or had that number been in her mind the whole time, buried there with other memories that she no longer paid any attention to. Her head was a lot like her closet, wasn't it? So filled and overflowing that it was difficult to find things sometimes. Yet he seemed to locate just what he wanted without trouble.

Thinking of him, she looked around for her man, noticing that the club was empty save for one lone client. There he sat, front row, center. Who was he tonight? A movie star? A model from the cover of one of her novels? No, this time he'd simply become a handsome patron of the exotic striptease arts. Casually dressed all in black, he had the look of someone who was ready to be aroused. He lifted his glass to her and nodded his approval at her performance. "Keep dancing for me."

Connie would. This was one of her most smutty fantasies, she'd always thought. Stripping for a lover. And not just doing some innocent little bedroom strip tease for a safe, cheerful audience of one. Bumping and grinding to encouraging chuckles of approval. No, she'd always day dreamed about actually working at a club, showing off her body, revealing herself. Now that it was actually happening, she put everything that she had in it. With an emphatic slowness, she moved to the beat, and sweetly, cleanly popped the clasp on her bra and let it fall free. Then she hooked her fingertips underneath the waistband of her panties. As soon as she did, she heard voices, and she glanced up startled as she saw the room was filled.

"What—" she began.

"That wasn't really your fantasy, was it?" the man murmured. In that watery, dream-like way, he was seated even closer. Right at her feet. "You lied when you said you wanted to strip at a club for one man only. No, baby. You forget how well I can see your true thoughts. You wanted to be on stage, for an audience. A group of rowdy, hungry men who have one thing on their minds." He gave a wave of his hand. "So here they are." Leaning forward, he slid one crisp green bill beneath the waistband of Connie's panties. His fingertips grazed the lips of her sex and she trembled. "Give it your best shot, honey. This one's for you."

Her cheeks were on fire, but she nodded. The man was right. Every time Connie had ever driven by the dive-bar Putty Tat, she'd imagined going in, performing for a band of strangers, even auditioning for some sleazy manager. Oh, she could see it. Standing in a faux-wood paneled back room. Tilting her head coyly as she began to undress. Feeling a man's eyes roaming over her. A man she'd never met before. A man who didn't care at all about her, who simply wanted to know what she looked like naked.

There was a thrill in that wasn't there? It had a naughty, dangerous quality that hummed beneath the surface.

She'd never set foot in a place like this, and even though she knew that Marla had occasionally visited strip bars with her different boyfriends, Connie wouldn't have thought to suggest it to her husband as something exotic to try for an evening out. She could just imagine the look on Ron's face. "With my wife? Are you totally nuts?"

But now, things were different. Now that she could actually make it happen, she took a deep breath and let loose. Her long blonde hair cascaded over her shoulders. Her small, perky breasts moved when she moved. The audience howled its approval as if with one voice, and Connie continued through the whole set feeling herself growing more aroused every second. As she'd always imagined it would be, dancing for a crowd of appreciative men was an absolute turn-on. The heat of their eyes on her spurred her desire to please. She rotated her hips, thrust them forward. With both hands, she held her naked breasts and lifted them up. The music flowed over her, flowed through her, and she moved effortlessly.

When the song ended, her panties were damp in the center and the dream lover joined her up on the stage, making the imaginary crowd disappear in a flash of neon light.

"The rest of the fantasy—" he said, obviously wanting to hear her say it for him.

"To do it up on stage."

"Show me."

She turned her back toward him and held onto the pole, bending forward at the waist and offering herself in this position. Gingerly, the man slid her panties down in back, leaving them on her thighs but lowered enough to give him access. His fingers trailed over her heart-shaped ass and then he pressed his own body to hers, driving smoothly inside of her. The two could see their reflections in the wall of mirrors and at a nod from the man's head the music came on again. This time, he chose a more melodious selection from the music in Connie's mind, "One" by U2. To this ballad, the man made love to her.

Beneath their feet, the lights continued to flicker on and off. Now, the colors were more muted. A pale jade-green square came to life replaced a second later by one colored a pastel blue, then a rose-pink, then a moonlit lavender. Velvety flower petals rained down from the ceiling, falling all around their moving bodies. Connie couldn't believe the difference in the sensations: screwing up on stage at a club was a hard-edged fantasy. But the way the man was taking her had a sweetness that rocked her from within.

"You're so unbelievably beautiful," the man said, gazing at their reflections as he thrust inside her. Connie's hands gripped onto the pole for support as she stared at her own image in the mirror on the wall. Multicolored lights shimmered. Connie's body glittered. Her eyes were half shut. Mouth half-open.

Another fantasy had come true.

# CHAPTER SIX

Ron was gone on his trip for nearly a week. Although she'd originally been dreading his absence, never truly comfortable being by herself even for an afternoon, this time was different. Connie spent those husbandless days swimming in the type of sexual ecstasy usually reserved for honeymooning couples or the erotic stars in adult movies. Once she'd returned from the eye-opening night in the motel, she didn't leave the house. Didn't take or make phone calls, except the standard check-ins from Ron.

Instead, she spent her time giving in to the most decadent fantasies she'd ever concocted. It was as if her dream man possessed a mental Rolodex and on each card was written a different sexual experience that she'd always wanted to try. Making love on a secluded mountaintop on a soft bed of grass; going at it in a very public place while people passed by; doing it in the shower after being shaved bare.

"Oh, man," he whispered during that interaction. "Oh, Connie.

You're so smooth down there." After shaving her, he'd gotten a hand mirror to show her what she looked like, and while she held the mirror in place, he'd started to kiss her. His tongue was warm against her newly shorn skin, and he spent long moments caressing each part. "Testing," he told her, "to see if I missed any stray curls." But he hadn't. She was smooth and sleek and the sex afterward had blown her mind. How bare she felt. How exposed. How truly naked.

"That's right," he'd said, reading her thoughts easily, as always. "You are naked to me. I can see everything, baby. You know that now, right? I can see your lovely shaved body. And I can see your naked, unedited thoughts. Get used to that, Connie. Stop trying to hide what you're thinking because it won't help."

She didn't question how this situation had happened, why she'd been transformed into some sort of an erotic channeler. She simply enjoyed what was going on. No, she'd never had recurring dreams before—but there was a first time for everything, right? And in this case, a second time and a third time.

The only rule, she learned, was that in order for their carnal connection to occur, she had to be asleep. Her dream lover couldn't come for her when she was awake, not even when she was touching herself and fantasizing about being with him. So she spent her days working hard to make herself tired: jogging for miles in the morning; using an exercycle at noon; organizing her outrageously disastrous closet; reading books that bored her but were "good" for her mind. It was the most productive week that she'd ever spent in many ways— most importantly in the way her dream lover made her come.

While still awake each day, Connie made a mental scorecard filled with her fantasies and every morning she checked off more. Sex on the beach—done that; making love on a cable car as it climbed the world-renowned hills of San Francisco—yes; screwing against the rear wall of a concert while a band played on—oh, yeah, did that twice.

4:00 PM Thursday. Dainty ceramic teapot nestled beneath a white crocheted warmer. Sterling silver service polished to a reflecting sheen. Antique lace tablecloth so fine it could tear if you looked at it too hard. Last place on earth you'd generally find Zachary.

His green eyes were wide open, and he tossed his long, glossy-black hair out of his face with an impatient shrug. "You're kidding, right?" he asked, visibly flinching when Marla told him what she wanted.

"An array of delicacies served to us in our own suite by a private waiter well-schooled in the age-old ritual of high tea," she continued, undaunted by his expression. She was repeating a passage from the slick brochure of one of San Francisco's most famous—and snobby—hotels. It was a passage that had indescribably turned her on.

Zachary just stared, dark brows arched incredulously. *What have they done with my girlfriend?* his expression said. *And who is this Martha Stewart-like impostor who has taken her place?*

"You won't regret it," she assured him, and he finally read the look in her eyes correctly, because he begrudgingly nodded his approval. Promised pleasure, Marla realized, will make people do the most unusual things.

4:15. Thursday. The tuxedo-wearing waiter had left, and Zachary was a true believer. Fantasy feast of finger-length cucumber and cream cheese sandwiches were ignored in favor of a far more decadent fantasy. Tiny teacakes sat iced so prettily all alone. And Marla's man was spread out on the richly carpeted floor tan slacks open, receiving his first-ever tea-flavored blowjob.

"Oh, God, Marla. Take another sip."

The fragrant liquid filled her mouth and she held it for a second, swishing slightly before swallowing. Then she was back down on him, her lips hot from the Earl Grey, the welcoming sensation of a pre-warmed mouth caressing his rock-hard erection. Sip, swallow, and suck. They could do this all day.

"Too good," Zachary groaned and arched his hips, pressing forward, gaining the contact he craved. "More. Please—"

Pinkie in the air, Marla drank again, taking her time to savor the flavor, a combination now of the strong tea and the hot-summertime taste of her boyfriend's naked skin. She was wearing sleek white gloves and a ruffled pastel party dress in place of her standard sexy animal-print uniform. But her soft red hair had come down from its too-tight bun, and she could feel that her perfectly applied lipstick had smeared. No outfit had ever excited her more.

Zachary's green eyes burned her with their heat as she swallow the tea, and then he stood, stripped out of his clothes, and got ready to really play. Gripping her shoulders, he moved her body so that she was on her back and he was positioned above, thrusting hard and slow into her willing, waiting mouth. She looked up at him, at the tribal tattoos that criss-crossed his broad biceps. He was comfortable cruising the steepest city hills on his Harley, or spread underneath his treasured old Chevy pick-up with his battered toolbox nearby. He was at ease in dangerous places that would scare every upper crust guest in this elite hotel.

And now he was turned on by teatime.

When his sex pressed against the back of her throat, she reached one hand up to stroke his body. The light caress of her still-gloved fingers took Zachary to a higher level.

"That, Marla," he whispered urgently. "Keep doing that."

Her fingertips made gentle circles as her mouth sucked harder. Careful rotations of soft fabric against even softer skin. The two differing sensations made Zachary close his eyes and moan, thrusting even harder and then holding still, sealing himself to her. She was growing wetter beneath the silly ruffles of the dress, and she glanced up from her position on the floor and saw pink-orange sunlight filtering through the scalloped lace edge of the tablecloth.

It was going to be a long afternoon.


"So what do you think?" Connie asked, twirling around in front of her dream lover, letting him see her long legs, her tight ass, her slim waist, all contained in a pair of new and tight-fitting jeans. They were in an anonymous dressing room in an anonymous store. She could hear the noises of shoppers around them. As always, the scenario was half-dreamy, half-real. Connie had the feeling that if she opened the door, she'd see a hallway of space. Nothingness out there beyond the containing walls of this make-believe dressing room.

"Really," Connie said, "Do you like them?"

The man didn't respond immediately, slowly taking in the way she looked. Sleek in her long-sleeved black blouse, her blonde hair up in a ponytail, green eyes wide while she waited for his answer.

"Tell me," she urged, tilting her head to look past him at her own reflection in the dressing room mirror. "Your honest opinion."

Still silent, he took one step toward her in the small space and grabbed hold of her hand. His fingers slid upward to close firmly around her delicate wrist, like a pair of handcuffs snapping shut. Something in the gesture made Connie forget what she was asking and pay attention to the looks he was giving her.

"Come here," he said, and she closed the space between them as he placed his free palm over the crotch of her jeans and let her feel his large hand against her. Instantly, she rested her sex on his hand, pressed into him, and he began to do the most intricate, marvelous things with his fingers. Dancing them up and down. Massaging her through the denim. Stroking just hard enough for her to lean her head back and sigh.

This was obviously the response he was looking for, and the dream lover quickly sat on the padded bench running the length of the room and he moved Connie so that she was cradled on his lap. Slowly, but firmly, he continued to rub her through the Levis. He paid attention to every touch, obviously on a mission. She helped, letting him know exactly what she wanted, pushing up with her hips to meet his stroking fingertips as he responded to each move. Focused on bringing her pleasure, he worked harder, firmer, then slid one finger between two buttons in the fly to touch her naked skin.

The feel of his hand on her was electrifying. Being fingered like this with her clothes still on made Connie feel the urgency in what they were doing. He pushed down, searching, and his fingertip plunged into the wetness that had already seeped through her nether lips. Withdrawing his hand, he licked his finger clean, then resumed his massage through her jeans.

Closing her eyes, Connie stifled a moan. It felt amazing. If he touched her just right with his middle finger, pressed it right up against the raised seam of her Levis, she could come. The dream lover understood this, and he sat her on one hand, and did exactly what she wanted. Tapping against her, harder as she got closer to climax, he stroked her until she was almost there. Almost—

"Take them off."

Connie opened her eyes, stunned at that point of almost coming that had made her brain slow down in direct correlation to the rate that her heart beat had speeded up.

"Just down to your knees. Now."

The urgency had her fumbling. She stood, a wreck, and tried to unbutton the jeans, but found her fingers useless. The dream lover did the job pulling hard and popping them open, then sliding the tight jeans down her lean thighs. He went on his knees in front of her, pressing his lips against her white panties, breathing her scent in through that sliver of cotton. Then these were pulled down, too, and he pushed her up against the cold glass of the dressing room mirror and licked at her with his eager, ready tongue.

Connie gripped onto the dream lover's shoulder, breathless, as he made those crazy spirals around her. She'd been on the brink from the decadent massage, and now the man was replicating those actions with his tongue. Around and around the tip went. Teasing and tricking, bumping up against her and then leaving that most magical place alone to throb desperately, urgently. He kissed her inner thighs for a moment, to give her a chance to miss him. Then, back at the game, he nudged her, pushing, before finally ringing her pulsing gem with his lips and sucking. Just sucking.

*Oh, yeah*, Connie thought, too tongue-tied to say the words out loud. *Oh, yeah*. Captured by the jeans and held upright by the dream lover's hands around her waist, she let her body relax into the climax. Sliding into it. Drifting into it. Helpless to stop herself. But then, she didn't want to stop. Did she?

When she opened her eyes, the dream lover was still helping — helping her take off her jeans. Then he was turning her, hands flat against the mirror his body behind her, letting her feel the promise of his sex pressed against her ass. Letting her know with a single look exactly what was going to happen next —

"Are you up for making drinks?" the dream lover asked Connie casually. She looked around the room, and saw that the mindset had once again been altered without her even sensing the transition. They were now in a deco-style bar, filled with customers from the jazz age. Women sparkled in beaded flapper-style gowns. Men looked sharp in zoot suits. Connie understood that these people didn't really exist. They were the human equivalent of a mirage, conjured up for her own pleasure.

Curious at her own transformation, she looked into a blue-tinted mirror that reflected the high-fashion room. She was in the same style dress as many of the women—a black, beaded-fringed number that swung when she walked.

"I know you like to read about different exotic recipes," the man continued. "Want to try one out for me?"

Connie nodded, and walked behind the polished black lacquered bar. She considered her choices before deciding to make a Singapore Sling, her preferred mixed drink. As was expected, because this was one of her fantasies, she found all the ingredients in a row in front of her: the gin and the cherry brandy and the lemon juice. The dream lover watched her measure out the correct quantity of each ingredient, watched her rotate the silver cocktail shaker, slow and steady, not fast or abrupt.

"You're turning me on," he said, his eyes focused on her. Again Connie looked at herself in the mirror, and now she saw that she was suddenly wearing a French maid's style costume, complete with tiny black lace apron. The dream lover looked at her with an odd expression, as if he were slightly disconcerted by her movements, turned on despite himself, and unsure why.

He came up behind her and put his arms around Connie's waist. She continued to do the cocktail dance, that enticing shimmy-shimmy shake and soon the dream lover had stripped out of his suit so that he was also naked, pressing against Connie. She moved slower, more seductively, not letting go of the beat.

"Keep it up," the dream lover said as he slid between her thighs, moving into the wet heat. "Don't stop."

Connie wasn't exactly sure what all that shaking would do to the Singapore Sling, but she did know what it would do to her. She grew wetter and wetter as the man pressed his lips to her ear crooning softly, "I like the way you move. You've got a good beat, and I can dance to it."

When Connie glanced around the room, she saw that the rest of the characters in this fantasy setting had mimicked their behavior. The men and women were undressed and maneuvering themselves into the most creative X-rated positions. Several couples were joined together, and Connie found her breath catching as she tried to mentally untangle the human puzzle before her. *They're not really here*, she reminded herself, but the man's voice answered that thought instantly.

"Then *you're* not really here."

And that didn't make sense because she could feel the man behind her. Could smell the scent of citrus and cherries. Could hear the echoing moans and sighs of the bar's other clientele.

As she tried to reconcile the situation within her mind, her dream lover started to pound into her, making up the music as he went along, finding a rhythm they could both get into and staying with it. Connie's breathing sped up and she finally had to set the shaker down and grip hold of the cool wood counter top to steady herself. The dream lover worked her at a more intense pace now, and Connie couldn't believe that she was going to come again. Yet there it was. Building, striving forward until she was panting and moaning, begging, "Please, oh, please."

"Please what?"

She didn't know what. He was doing everything she wanted, but she had the need to ask for more of it. "Please do me. Harder. Harder."

And he drove in deeper, until his hips were pressed solidly with Connie's ass and his chest was pushed into her back.

"Like this?" he murmured his fingers on her arms again, digging in, holding Connie steady. The dream lover's rod slipped out only an inch or so, only the base, leaving the head deep inside her and then pushing right back in again.

"Is this what you like?" he asked, "The shaft?" Now he pulled out almost completely. "Or the head?" He rubbed back and forth pulling out entirely and then slipping back inside. "Head?" he asked, and then slid back inside her again, "Or shaft?"

Connie couldn't tell. She didn't know. She liked it all. She just didn't want it to stop.

It did. He expected an answer. Until he got one, he stayed entirely still, inside her body but not moving, not giving her the motion she craved. Connie's muscles gripped uselessly. Yes, it felt good to be filled, but she needed the dance steps to make her come.

"The head," she said, and he pushed in and out, in and out, just that thick rounded portion, until she said, "the shaft," and he rocked the whole thing in her to the hilt. She was nearly weeping, realizing that he wanted her to keep directing him, needing only one thing: to come. Needing that more than anything else in the world. It was amazing how consumed you could get when you were on the verge, Connie realized, when your partner had the patience to keep you on that verge until you thought you might literally go insane.

"Head," she said softly pleading, and he gave her that part, again pulling out to press it against the gates of her sex, digging in so that she felt flames of heat lick up and down her body, startling contractions that made her close her eyes and grip her hands even tighter against the ridge of the counter.

"Now, the shaft," the dream lover said, gracefully taking over when he realized Connie just might not be able to speak any more. In and out he went, until his tool was well-slicked with the sweetness of Connie's arousal. Until the smell of her sex scent was all around them in the kitchen, overpowering the fresh citrus fragrance of the half-made Slings.

"Shaft, then head," the man said, making his voice match the beat of his body. When he came, he pulled out entirely and reached for a bottle of virgin olive oil that had suddenly appeared on the counter. In a blink, while Connie was lost in the haze of almost-coming the room had changed. Not just the appearance of the oil, but the entire bar had transformed into a fancy restaurant kitchen. Steel refrigerators. Tiled counters. Hardwood floors. He was plucking images from her mind as soon as they appearedthere, and now, he was going to make another one of her sticky-sweet fantasies come true.

Connie turned to watch him oil up the tip of his sex with it, watched him slick the tool all over with that golden liquid. "Bend over," he said, "we're not finished yet."

She didn't hesitate. She bent over at the waist, grabbed hold of her ankles, and waited. In this most vulnerable position, she wished she were blindfolded, wished her hands were cuffed, her ankles tied. It was so difficult to stand there on her own, to wait patiently until he was ready. So why didn't he help her out? Why didn't he read her thoughts and make them come true?

Because she didn't really want any of those things, did she? The power of submission turned her on. Forcing herself to stay the way he wanted her to was even more exciting than if he'd made her to behave for him. But finally, just as she thought about straightening up, about turning around, he entered her slippery wet sex and pushed once more, softly. Connie sighed, trying to adjust herself to the sensation. Trying and failing. He gripped into her waist, holding her, waiting ever so patiently for her to ask him to continue. When she remained silent, he whispered, "head or shaft?"

"Shaft," she said. The dream lover grabbed the bottle of oil again from the counter and poured it in a river between her thighs. He stepped back, pulling out, and liberally oiled her, lubing her up with the olive oil, the fragrance all around them.

Then he put his rod where it had been before, saying, "head," as he slipped it in, and then "shaft" as he slid in the rest of the tool.

Connie couldn't speak any more. The feeling of being filled was too intense. She let the dream lover tell her how he was going to do her, listened to the words describing each action. He knew how to move. After the first stroke, he began to press in deep.

"Head," he said, "then shaft." He spoke these words, that didn't mean much, but listening to them calmed her, let her focus on the overwhelming need to come, and when he told her to touch herself, to put her fingers between her legs and pleasure herself, she immediately did. She moaned, stroking herself between her legs, wanting only release. The combination of all the different actions worked together to take her closer to the edge, closer to the finish line where she would win—dirty, and naked, and sinful, but satisfied.

The dream lover finally gripped into her waist, arching forward and calling out her name. Then he came. The sound of an animal behind her, that almost unearthly sound of reaching the final pleasure point, drove Connie over the edge with him.

Afterward, he pulled out and held Connie in his arms, olive oil still on his palms. Gilding her. In the gleaming rays of sun from a skylight overhead, they looked like statues come to life, both coated in the golden liquid. Not human but majestic, fantasy turned to reality.

Sprawled naked on her bed, on the last night of Ron's trip, Connie waited for her lover to arrive. She had candles lit, soft music by Sade playing in the background. Everything was perfect. Yes, she knew that when she met him in that mental set, it wouldn't matter what her bedroom looked like. He'd whisk her away to some far off location, found only in the deep recesses of her mind. But she'd discovered that setting the stage for romance in real life helped her to fall asleep more quickly. Made her that much more ready for a rendezvous with him.

Simply the idea of what they might do together this evening had her totally aroused. Would he see from her thoughts how ready she was? There were so many more ways she wanted to play. Maybe she'd be able to talk this time. Maybe he wouldn't have to read her mind, but she'd be able to actually get the words out. She tried to imagine what that would be like. Speaking her desires. Hearing the fantasies spelled out in her own voice.

But she couldn't sleep. And without sleep, he couldn't come for her.

"Please—" she murmured looking at the clock. The numbers flashed over, one then another. She was mesmerized by the green glow. "I'm so tired. Let me sleep."

Nothing.

# CHAPTER SEVEN

Sunlight shone down on Connie's small, cottage-style house. The storm, now several days in the past, was only a distant memory. Connie's silver car pulled into the driveway, but she sat in the driver's seat for a moment, gathering her thoughts and belongings. She stepped out of the car, wearing one of her standard teacher's outfits—tan slacks, pale blue sweater set and sensible black penny loafers with shiny pennies in their slits. Her arms held a day's worth of school materials, and her shoulders sagged under the weight.

As she walked to the front door, she saw her best friend curled up on the step, reading a copy of *Cosmopolitan* magazine. "Marla," Connie said, surprised. "What are you doing here?"

"At least you haven't forgotten my name."

"What's that supposed to mean?" Connie asked, trying to sound lighthearted.

Marla sighed and stood up, setting the magazine down on top of her sequined purse. She straightened the seams in her fire engine-red stockings and then smoothed out the wrinkles in her ebony dress. Marla always dressed with a flair. Today, sparkling rhinestone barrettes twinkled in her curly hair, holding those usually untamable tresses in place. "I must have left ten messages on your answering machine this week. Plus, I talked to Ron three times since he got home, and you know he's not my favorite conversation partner. I'm starting to feel as if you're angry with me. Are you mad that I made fun of your dream lover at lunch?"

"Of course, I'm not," Connie said, shocked at the thought.

"Then why haven't you called me back?"

Without answering, Connie opened the door and together the women entered the house. Connie set her bundles down on the coffee table then brushed a stray wisp of golden hair out of her gray-green eyes.

"You look different," Marla said, gazing up and down at Connie. The clothes were the same style as always—refined and restricted, nothing shocking or even particularly hip for the six-year-olds. But Connie exuded a glow that had always eluded her in the past. She looked Marla decided, satisfied. This was a look Marla knew intimately from her own post-coital reflection in the mirror, but she'd never seen Connie so radiant.

"You know how it is. First week of school everything gets crazy. Then Ron came home after being gone for days and we had to spend time catching up. I was going to call you this weekend—" This sounded lame to both of them, and Connie felt herself stammer to a halt without the will to continue. It simply wasn't like her to lie to her best friend.

Marla studied Connie closely. "There's something else. Something you're just not telling me, and I can't figure it out."

"Like what?" Connie asked, "like I'm leading a secret double-life and the government won't let me come clean with my friends?" But even as she joked, a note of guilt was apparent in her voice.

"Like how am I supposed to know? I'm not a psychic. I just know you've never avoided me before. Not even when I told you how I felt about Ron before you got married. And that's what you were doing. Don't deny it."

The women stared at each other for a long, silent moment.

"Okay," Connie said, sitting down. "Okay. You're right. There was something. But it's too dumb to bother talking about. And it's over." She said this last part somewhat sadly.

"What's over?"

Connie opened her mouth to explain, then stopped, shaking her head. There was no way to tell Marla what had happened to her without sounding as if she'd gone crazy. Frustrated, she turned away. Marla sat at her side on the sofa, holding her hand. "Is it about Ron?"

"No, not at all. Not really."

"Come on, kiddo. Tell me. This is Marla, remember?" She widened her lovely blue eyes at Connie, making an exaggerated face. "Just think of all the dirt you know about me. More blackmail fodder than anyone else has out there."

Connie laughed and then leaned back into the deep velvety pillows. She took a deep breath, preparing to tell all. The relief of having someone to share with pulsed through her. "He came back."

"Who?"

"My dream lover. That night, after you and I had lunch."

"But you told me that you never have the same dream twice."

"This time, I did. More than that, actually. It was a continuation, like a sequel. Or a serial, really. A mini-series."

"So?"

"It's completely over-the-top. You're going to laugh at me."

"Connie, remember the time I liked that British guy? And I didn't know what to do to make him like me back? So I gave him a..."

"A lock of your hair. I know, you were a nut case over Jackson."

"This can't possibly be worse than that, can it?"

Staring at the floor, Connie started to talk. She spoke very quickly, as if speed would help get everything out that she needed to say. "Every time I closed my eyes, he was there. Taunting me. Telling me the different things he was going to do when we got together. And the thing is, I wanted it. I wanted to give in, but I wasn't able to."

"Not even in your dreams?" Marla asked, shocked at the thought.

Connie shook her head. "I just couldn't take the pressure from him. I felt as if I was losing my mind, and I ran out of the house and drove around in circles. At some point, really late, I tried to call you but your machine was on. So then I just drove and drove. Got coffee. Nearly got into an accident with an 18-wheeler."

"Good lord, Connie, what were you thinking?"

"I wasn't thinking. I just wanted to get away."

Marla's expression was confused. "I still don't understand that. You wanted to get away from your dream?"

Connie nodded, pitifully.

"So what did you do?"

"I ended up at a motel. But he found me there."

"Found you—"

Connie was insistent. "That's what it was like. I know it was all in my head, but he *found* me."

"So, in this dream did he—?"

Connie nodded.

"And did you—?"

She nodded again.

"And was it good?"

"Oh, god, Marla. It was unreal."

Marla stared at Connie, but said nothing. This easily explained

Connie's altered appearance. Marla knew all about the strength of a world-shattering orgasm.

"I mean, it was better than good. It was better than it's ever been with Ron. Then it's ever been with anyone. Even Marco in college—" Connie began to cry softly and Marla put her arms around her friend and held on.

"He really made you come, didn't he?"

Connie nodded.

"It's hard to let those guys go. They're definitely rare." Marla sighed, as if remembering someone wonderful. "But don't worry, Connie. The right man, with the right touch—"

Connie interrupted her. "That was five days ago. And for the whole time Ron was gone, he came to me, every night, every nap. I gave up coffee for those days, walking around in a daze. I worked out until I was exhausted. You wouldn't have believed it if you saw me. I literally have never tried so hard to go to sleep before. And then, on the last night, he just stopped visiting. It was as if he knew that Ron was coming back home the next day, or something. He was punishing me—I don't know. I truly don't know. I've tried to find him, tried to call him back to me, but I can't."

"What did I say about men?"

Connie tried to laugh. "Marla, it was amazing. He knew everything I've ever wanted to do. And he made all of my fantasies reality."

"Of course, he knew," Marla explained patiently. "Just like you said before, he wasn't real, Con. He's some fantasy man you created to take care of you in a way that Ron doesn't. And he hasn't come back because you feel too guilty to give in to your wants and needs when Ron's around. You don't think he'd approve."

"It didn't feel like a dream."

"Everyone's had dreams like that. But you woke up, and that's it.

He's not coming back any more because you don't need him. Now, you need to deal with what your dream was telling you."

Connie closed her eyes and shivered.

"There's more, isn't there?"

"The day after the dream, I received a bouquet of my favorite flowers and a note signed 'from your admirer.'"

"They were from Ron, right?"

"The last time Ron sent me flowers? It was when I had my tonsils out."

"Are you sure they weren't from him? I mean, did you ask?"

"No."

"Why not?"

"They were the same flowers in the dream."

A motorcycle pulled into the gravel drive. Marla stood to look out the window. "I hate to leave now," she said, "But Zach's here to get me. I told him I needed to talk to you before we went out tonight. He's playing over at the Lover's Lounge, and I'm going with him for rehearsal. But we can talk tomorrow."

Connie nodded, obviously on the verge of tears.

"I don't know what's going on, Connie. But I'm sure there's a rational explanation." Marla took a deep breath, preparing to say something truly serious. "Look, I know what it's like to be confused about a relationship, and I think that's how you're feeling. Your subconscious is obviously trying to tell you something. And listen, next time you have a problem...."

"Like a bad dream?"

"Like anything. I want you to call me—and leave a message. Or come over. Don't keep it bottled up. Okay? That's not healthy. I want you to promise me you'll never avoid me again."

Connie nodded. Marla moved toward the door. "You were smart not to say anything about this to Ron. We both know what he's like." As she hurried out the door toward Zach on his Harley, Ron pulled his black Mercedes sedan into the driveway. He glared angrily at Marla as she passed him.

"Hi Ron," Marla cooed.

Ron said nothing.

"Bye, Ron."

Ron entered the living room to find Connie sitting there daydreaming.

"I suppose she knows everything."

Ron's icy tone brought Connie back to the present. "About what?"

"About him?"

"Him who?" Connie asked, her voice wavering.

"Your god damn lover, that's who." He glared at her angrily as he spoke, and a vein in his forehead pulsated with the intensity of his emotions. Connie had never seen him look this ferociously upset before, and she stared at her husband, stunned.

"I..."

"Don't waste your breath lying to me, Connie. I've got the proof. What I want to know now are reasons. Haven't I taken good care of you? Provided for you?" He gestured with outstretched arms to the well-decorated living room. "Given you a good home. A nice life."

"Honestly, I don't know what you're talking about," Connie said, but her eyes glanced over at the bouquet of flowers on the bookshelf.

Ron pulled a letter from his pocket and read aloud: "Ron Morris, your wife cheated on you. I know this for a fact because I'm the man who slept with her. She is very good in bed. Her passionate screams really turned me on."

"Ron, this is not true—"

"The letter goes on, Connie. 'Don't believe me? Here are the facts:

It happened last week when you were in Washington selling your franchises. I'm sure that your sweet wife will deny this ever happened. She wouldn't want to damage your over-working ego. So check with the Creekside Motel. That's where we spent the night. The generous girl even paid for the room with her VISA card. Very easy for you to verify. Better keep your eyes on her, Ronny-boy. She's hot."

Looking agitated, Connie began to pace the room. "This is a bad joke."

"Is this 'bad joke' true?"

"How can you even ask that? You *know* me." Connie ran her hands through her long hair, pulling loose the ponytail and then snapping the elastic around her wrist. Nervously, she twirled her fingers through the ends of her hair, and Ron grabbed one hand and held it tightly.

"You're not denying it, then?"

"There's nothing to deny—"

"The facts, Connie."

"I don't understand why anyone would write such a thing."

"Maybe your lover had something you apparently don't have. It's called a conscience."

"That's not what I'm missing, Ron," Connie said, finally getting angry. "What I'm missing is two-fold: a phantom love and a husband who trusts me."

"This is what I want to know. Did you spend all night with a man at the Creekside Motel?"

"No."

"How about half the night?" he sneered. "You've got to come clean with me, Connie. How long has this been going on?"

"Stop interrogating me. Nothing happened."

"Christ, you're impossible. I called the motel."

"You really don't trust me at all, do you?"

"You were there. I checked with VISA. Yep, that charge will appear on the next bill. I talked to someone at the front desk at the Creekside. Not only do they remember you arriving in an agitated state they heard you moaning, Connie. The couple in the next room even complained about the noise. That's in the log book."

"It's not what you think. I'll tell you what I know. But you have to believe me."

Furious, Ron gestured for her to reveal her story. Connie winced, knowing somehow that this wasn't going to play out any better with Ron than it had with Marla—and there was much more at stake. Still, she took a deep breath and gave it her best shot. "The night you packed for your trip, I dreamed a man was here in our bed with me."

"What kind of nonsense is this?"

Connie rushed on. "Only it wasn't here. It was some place nearby. . . or far away. I don't know. And this man touched me, in the dream. *Just* in the dream. And wanted me to..." As with Marla, she couldn't fully explain what happened. What the dream lover wanted, or what he was capable of. She remembered it all in a rush: the stripping fantasy, the Ferris wheel ride, being a bad girl. "I escaped from him. I mean, I woke up, yet it felt as if I was breaking free of his hold. But the next night, when you were gone, he came back. He knew everything, Ron. It was so scary. I ran from the house and drove on the freeway. I was almost killed. I ended up at that motel not far from Carmel, but it was just me in the room. All by myself. I tried to stay awake, but eventually I fell asleep."

"And?"

Connie started to cry.

"And you two did it."

"It was only a dream, Ron. I swear."

"You and some stranger screwing like bunnies in a low-class

motel while your trusting husband was out of town slaving away on a business trip." He shook his head angrily. "How totally cliché. You could get a job writing for a soap opera, Connie. You have the plot down fast."

"You're not even listening to me."

"What did he look like?"

"I couldn't see his face. It kept changing. Sometimes he was somebody I recognized. Other times he was a stranger."

"But the man, this dream man had sex with you."

Connie nodded.

"And you were—as he so eloquently said—very good? Very good in bed. But it was just a dream? *This* is the story you expect me to believe? Is this the alibi you and that idiot friend of yours were concocting when I came home? What do you think I am, a moron?" Ron pointed to the letter. "How about this letter. Is this also part of a dream?" Ron moved close to Connie and shook the crisp white piece of paper in her face. She flinched and tried to move away from him, but he grabbed her wrist and held on. "Maybe I'm dreaming right now. Maybe I'm dreaming that we're having this insane conversation. Perhaps, I'm fast asleep upstairs having sex with my own dream lover. Maybe *I'm* the one who's very, very good."

"Then you would be dreaming," Connie spat, snatching the letter from her husband's hand and ripping it into pieces. She'd had enough. Her nerves vibrated with tension.

"You can't tear up the truth, Connie." Grabbing her shoulders, he shook her. "This isn't a dream. This is real life. And that ripping sound? That was the sound of your marriage coming apart in your hands."

Connie pulled away from her husband, snatched up her purse and car keys, and ran from the house. Ron bent down and started picking up the tiny pieces of the letter.

# CHAPTER EIGHT

"Where is everybody?" Marla asked, looking around the deserted club. Chairs were still standing upside-down on top of the small, wooden tables. The bar was empty, and the stage entirely bare except for several microphone stands and amplifiers. It was obvious that the wait staff hadn't arrived yet to set the place up. "I thought you guys were doing a sound check."

"Yeah, we are," Zach nodded, leaning against the lip of the stage. He had on a black long-sleeved shirt with a barbed wire design imprinted in blood red running across the chest, and his long dark hair was down, framing his face. Zach's band was called 'Dirty White Pants,' but the snow-white slacks that Zach had on were currently still clean. By the end of the evening, they'd match the band's moniker.

Quietly, Zach waited to see when Marla would understand his intentions for the evening. But his lady was still busy looking at the framed notices on the walls—posters for bands who had played the club in the past. She didn't pick up on the vibe her boyfriend was giving out. Not until she caught the movement from the corner of her eye. Zach was stripping out of his clothes. Boots off. White jeans down. Shirt tossed aside.

"The sound check's not for hours, is it?" Marla asked, suddenly realizing exactly what was going on.

He glanced at his watch. "45 minutes, actually. I have the key here. The staff doesn't show up until seven, and the rest of the guys will be late, I'm sure. You know how musicians are."

Marla smiled at him as she pulled her dress over her head. Yes, she knew just how musicians were. Beneath the tight black dress, she had on only crimson stockings, a lace garter, and a leopard-print bra.

"You're mismatched," Zach said, noticing the two different patterns in her underwear.

"I like to be unpredictable," Marla smiled, moving toward him.

"So do I," Zach said, lifting her easily in his arms and setting her up on the stage. "So do I."

Connie needed Marla. Desperately, she tried to remember where the club was. Lover's Lounge. Was that downtown or over the bridge in Marin somewhere? Her head hurt from the fight with Ron, and she tried to figure out her options. Definitely, she would go see Marla. She had no other choice, did she? But she wouldn't drive wildly as she had on the night that the dream lover first came for her. She'd be more controlled.

Stopping at a pay phone, she got out the phone book and looked up the address of the club.

Zachary wanted to do his own sort of sound check. A sound check based on Marla's cries of sexual satisfaction. He sat his stripped-down girlfriend on an over-sized speaker, and gave her the first instruction. "Now, spread your legs and close your eyes."

She shot him a look, not obeying immediately. But when he just stood there and waited, Marla slowly shut her eyes and parted her lean legs. Zachary moved quickly to the instrument panel and turned on a tape he'd brought with him. The mighty bass vibrations pulsed through Marla's body and she gasped at the intensity of the feeling. This was a bit like the time they'd screwed on top of the washing machine in her apartment complex, getting off during the endless rinse cycle. They'd fed quarter after quarter into the mouth of the machine. Her clothes had never been so clean.

Now, to the music of Zach's own band, Marla felt her body turning on from within. Zach watched for a moment, loving the way his girlfriend looked when she was aroused. Her whole body changed. Her cheeks turned a deep rosy pink. Her lips parted hungrily. Her back arched, breasts lifted upward. Even the rhythm of her breathing changed. She was gulping the air in tremulous gasps, perched on the edge of the amp, waiting for him to claim her.

When he could put it off no longer, he came forward, pressed into her, and he sighed as those rumbling vibrations throbbed from her body to his.

"Oh, yeah," Marla sighed, wrapping her slender legs around his flat waist. "That's right."

He gripped into her, pulling her hard against him, closing his eyes as his body melded with hers. Being inside Marla was overwhelming—how their two bodies merged together. Marla's skin shined in the stage lights, seeming almost to sparkle. Her red curls bounced each time he thrust forward, jubilant in their movement. Zach kept his eyes open the whole time. He wanted to memorize everything, to remember each nuance of this event. Because later, when the club filled up with employees and customers, he'd recall every detail of what they had done earlier in the evening, and it would give him an extra charge remembering

Marla's naked body astride the speaker. The sexy memory would sound in his voice, echo in the way he moved with his band. Some of his band members didn't like to do it before a gig, thinking that climaxing over-relaxed them and made them forget how to play their instruments. Zach disagreed with that belief. Satisfaction always worked through him like a powerful mood-enhancing drug. When he got laid right before a show, his performances were always enhanced. He wondered if a reviewer would ever catch on to that sexy secret. "Don't go to a show of Dirty White Pants if lead-singer Zach is single. His sexual desperation will negatively effect his creativity."

Playing music on stage had been Zach's fantasy since he was little. But sex on stage was his all-time favorite way to play.

By the time Connie arrived at the club, the rest of the band members were milling about and Marla had gathered herself together. She appeared slightly mussed at the edges, but it was a look that worked for her. Bright eyes, pink cheeks, lipstick kissed away leaving only the stain of it on her full mouth.

A crowd of eager customers poured steadily through the doorway. They were mostly young, San Francisco hipsters wearing lots of black and sporting many piercings and body modification art. Connie stood out noticeably against the music enthusiasts in her teacher duds and tailored style. Marla saw Connie standing in the doorway, insecure, eyes red and still watery, and she instantly ran to her side.

"Ron—" Connie said, before she started to cry again.

"Don't worry, kiddo," Marla told her stroking Connie's long blonde hair. "Whatever it is, we'll fix it. We'll fix everything."

# CHAPTER NINE

The decor in Marla's apartment perfectly reflected her lifestyle. Just like in her clothing store in the city's Haight/Ashbury district, the ambiance she'd created in the small rooms conjured an image of a serious vixen. Velvet was the dominating fabric, red and leopard-print the dominating colors and patterns. Beaded silk wall-lamps lit the room in an enchanting glow. A plush rug with golden fringe covered nearly the entire living room floor, and covering nearly the entire rug were the contents of Marla's closet. As usual, her apartment looked as if a cyclone had whirled its way through, leaving a terrible mess in its wake. A colorful medley of delicate clothes was strewn on chairs: dainty antique slips, crocheted cardigans, the form-fitting silky dresses that she favored. An empty wine bottle lay pointing due north on the floor. Tabloid newspapers decorated the coffee table with their bold, screaming headlines.

Connie curled under a blush-colored blanket on the sofa, face up, eyes open. She stared at Sushi, Marla's pet calico cat, who gazed back at her with unblinking jade green eyes. Marla entered the room, carrying two steaming cups of coffee. She brushed the cat aside and set the mugs in their places.

"I'm so glad you found me at the club last night," she said. "It was right for you to come and not be on your own."

"Thanks, Marla," Connie said, lifting her cup and blowing on the hot liquid.

"So did you sleep okay?"

"Like the dead," Connie sighed.

"Any nightmares?"

"None. Total blackout."

"No dream lovers?"

Connie shook her head. Her tousled blonde mane fell forward, and she shrugged impatiently to push the hair out of her eyes.

"Now we'll never know if he's the one who sent the letter to Ron." No, Marla still didn't fully believe in Connie's explanation of events, but she couldn't let her friend down.

"As if that's all I have worry about." Connie sipped her coffee and then, taking mental stock of her situation, started to cry helplessly. Marla took the mug from her hand and moved in close on the sofa to give her a hug. "I can't go home," Connie whimpered. "I don't have a home anymore."

"You can stay here. For as long as you like, Con. You know that. Anything I have is yours. You understand that, right?"

Connie surveyed the mess and then laughed through her tears. "This place isn't big enough for two grown-up slobs."

"We managed in college," Marla reminded her. "We can do it again. Besides, I predict that Ron'll come crawling to you when he realizes how much he misses you. How much he needs you. I give him—" Marla looked over at the black Elvis clock on the wall, its legs swishing back and forth to tick off the seconds, "I don't know.

Six hours and seventeen minutes before he comes to his senses."

"I wish—"

"Do you, Connie?" Marla interrupted. "You know what they say about wishing." To soften the statement, Marla added, "And besides, while you're waiting for Ron to calm down, we can have fun being bachelorettes again."

"I hate to be a burden on you—"

Marla rummaged in a drawer until she found a spare key dangling on a silvery chain.

"Trust me. It'll work. Here's the key. No deposit needed."

Connie shook her head. Like a comic book hypnotist, Marla swung the key back and forth in front of her friend's open eyes. "Take it. Take it. Take it."

Connie laughed again. Pretending to be under Marla's spell, she took the key. "I don't have anything to wear, Marla. I left so angry I didn't even pack a bag. And now Ron won't answer the phone. I tried last night when we got back from the club. He's got the machine on, and he won't take my calls. I don't—"

"Worry is what you don't have to do. I own a clothes store. Remember?" Marla gestured to the various items of frilly clothing draped over every available surface. "We'll give you a make-over and then we'll celebrate by going out after work."

"It's a school night, Marla. I can't."

"But you will," Marla said in her faux-hypnotist's voice. "You will. You will. Now, go and take your shower."

"Yes, Mistress," Connie grinned. She headed for the bathroom. In the living room, Marla picked up a tabloid newspaper and studied it seriously, as if the gossip rag were the *New York Times*.

At the end of a long, tiring day at school, Connie stopped at the nearest ATM to pick up cash. If she and Marla were going out on the town, she'd need money. She planned on treating her friend to an evening of fun. But when she tried to punch her code into the automatic teller, a message flashed: CARD CANCELED.

Connie re-inserted her card and entered the numbers a second time, certain that in her dazed state of mind she had typed in the wrong code. Again, an error message alerted her to the fact that the account had been canceled.

"Ron!" Connie spat. "Oh, Jesus." The account held her money as well as his. What right did he have to make her life difficult? She rushed to a nearby pay phone and made a call. After listening for a moment, she slammed the receiver down and headed to her car. Inside, her anger left her and she looked defeated again.


Marla and Connie went to their favorite club near Marla's apartment, Savoire Faire. Marla looked glorious as usual in a wrap-around dress made of emerald green silk. Connie was wearing a pair of Marla's animal-print slacks and a black turtleneck sweater. She had let her hair down—literally—and it cascaded over the cashmere turtleneck like spun gold.

Although she'd had her doubts, Connie had let her friend convince her that a night on the town was what she most needed. And maybe Marla was right. Connie relaxed alongside her best friend, preparing for her tequila ritual. Focusing on the glass, she took a breath, let it out, then lifted her shot and downed it in one practiced swallow.

"Why have you stayed with him for so long?" Marla asked. It was a question she'd wanted to pose to Connie for years, but had never had the guts.

"We're married, Connie said." Her voice wasn't affected by the liquor—not from just one shot—but she already felt more relaxed.

"That's not an answer."

"I love him—"

"Do you?" Marla asked. "Do you really?"

Connie shrugged. "I thought I did. The way he acted when he got that letter—that was unexpected. Ron's always been jealous, I guess. But I thought that was how he showed his appreciation. The fact that he didn't want other men looking at me."

"Jealousy isn't the same thing as love," Marla said, realizing as she spoke that she sounded like the type of message found in a fortune cookie.

"I know that," Connie sighed. "OK, so the real answer to your question? It's this—I don't know."

"Do you think that he might have been the one to send the letter?"

"That doesn't make any sense."

"Maybe he was testing you. He could have gotten the VISA bill, seen the motel charge on it, and decided to mess with you. Sort of like a test. He guessed you were cheating, and he wanted to see your reaction."

"Well, he saw my reaction, all right. I totally freaked out at him."

"But that's what you would have done if you were innocent, right?" Marla asked.

"Or guilty," Connie said, motioning to the bartender that they were ready for another round.

A yellow cab pulled up in front of Marla's building and the two friends staggered out. Unsteadily, the women climbed the stairs and approached the door of Marla's apartment.

"I told you we'd have fun," Marla said, slurring slightly.

"We were just smart not to drive home," Connie said, trying to keep her eyes focused on the task of walking forward in a straight line. The walls kept coming out to bump against her, despite her carefully placed steps.

"I just hope we'll remember where my car is in the morning."

Connie rummaged through her purse. "We'll be lucky if we find our keys." The women giggled, and Marla opened her fringed leather purse and poured the contents onto the woven straw welcome mat. Connie did the same. Sifting through the debris, Marla found her house keys. With a bit of effort, she swept her various possessions, and several of Connie's, back into her bag and opened the door to the apartment. Inside, Marla gestured for Connie to follow. Connie did, probing into the contents of her own purse.

"Twenty-four dollars and twelve cents. That's it until payday a week and a half from now. Goddamn him."

Marla slumped onto a soft chair and closed her eyes while Connie fell onto the red velvet sofa across the room.

"Ron?" Marla asked, eyes still shut.

"No," Connie muttered. "The other one."

"Your dream lover?"

"Doesn't make sense, does it?"

"Seems to me that your real problem is Ron. He's the jerk-off who canceled your credit card and put a hold on the checking account." Now that she was drunk, Marla was even less cautious in her appraisal of Connie's husband.

"Ron's always been like that. Always. You remember the time I had that student teacher in my class?"

"Refresh my memory."

"Ron was convinced that the two of us were doing it together. I don't know what he thought, that we headed off into the cloakroom at recess, or something. At least, he was jealous until the man came onto Ron at our school's Open House. Then he was just intensely weirded out."

Marla laughed. "I'd have liked to have seen that. Ron must have been absolutely floored by having his masculinity challenged."

"But this is different," Connie said seriously. "This wouldn't have happened without the letter. I have to find out who sent it and why. I know in my heart that it wasn't Ron. And I just can't make sense of the situation. It's all a big mess in my brain. Not helped by the tequila, I must say."

"So what are you going to do? Hire a private eye?"

"Yeah. As soon as we find one willing to work for twenty-four bucks."

"Don't forget the twelve cents," Marla murmured, on the verge of sleep.

"If I could just figure it out. I mean, this letter obviously came from a real person. Someone who knows me and knows Ron. Someone who might have seen me go to the motel, who was following me. But who could that have been? The boy at the donut shop? No, that doesn't make sense. Maybe the man who checked me into the room—" Connie looked up to see whether Marla was following her reasoning. It sounded good so far, right? But she noticed that her friend had fallen asleep.

She got up and threw a tiger-striped blanket over her Marla, then collapsed again on the sofa and closed her eyes. The apartment was quiet. Light from a passing car slid across the golden sponge-printed wall. In her dream, Connie stood in a circle of light. The bed was gone. The flowers were gone. No music played. She peered into the inky darkness. "Are you here?" Connie asked tentatively. "I really need to talk to you."

What tricks was she lacking to make him appear? She thought hard. Dorothy had to click her sparkling ruby heels three times to get what she wanted. What other ways were there to make magic occur? She tried to remember advice from the book Marla had lent her, visualizing her sexual energy spreading throughout her body.

Nope. Nothing.

As if there was no barrier between sleeping and waking, Connie sat up on Marla's sofa and looked around. In the darkness, she fumbled for the switch on a nearby lamp, then checked the clock over the mantle. She frowned at the late hour, then rubbed her forehead, thinking.

An idea began to form in her mind. Would it work? She didn't know, but she decided to take a chance. Quietly, she stood up and went to Marla's bookshelf. She chose a romance from the assorted novels displayed. She'd been reading a similar one the night she'd first encountered the dream lover. Lying back on the sofa, she read for a few moments, smiled to herself and then closed her eyes.

Back in the circle of light, Connie turned around and around. "Where are you?" But in response to her query, there was only a deep, lonely silence.

# CHAPTER TEN

Light streamed through the large window across from the sofa. Marla, still slumped in the over-stuffed leather chair, opened her eyes slowly and tentatively lifted her head up, testing the strength of her hangover.

*Ooh, bad.*

She winced, stayed still for another moment, then tried again. She needed something. Water. Aspirin. Another shot of tequila to quiet the noise in her head. What had she been thinking? That was easy to answer. She hadn't been thinking at all. She'd simply wanted to get Connie to relax and have a good time. The hangover was definitely worth the fun they'd shared over shots of tequila.

When she turned toward the left, she saw Connie, already awake, staring up at the ceiling. Connie looked exactly as awful as Marla felt. No, on second thought, Marla realized that she looked far worse. "My god. What's wrong with you? Was it the last round of drinks?"

Connie shook her head.

"Oh, no," Marla gasped, gaining more momentum. "Did your dream lover come back?"

"I waited for him all night. The room had changed, but he was there. I could feel him watching me. But he wouldn't show himself, wouldn't answer when I spoke. I don't know why. It was as if he were just watching me for the fun of it. Like it was some sort of twisted mind game."

"Maybe you should call for a substitute today," Marla suggested. "Take it easy. Hang out in the apartment and gather your thoughts together."

Connie got up and headed for the bathroom. "Don't worry about me. I'm fine. I'm just fine."

Marla watched her friend walk down the hall, then shook her head. It was obvious that Connie was far from fine.

Connie moved around her classroom from child to child, offering her steady, calming influence on her youthful students. The children were drawing houses and apartments, showing where they lived—all except one six-year-old named Neal who was creating a mural-sized work of an army tank with guns blazing. He'd used every shade of green and brown there was in order to make a realistic camouflage pattern.

"We're drawing our homes today, Neal," Connie sighed, looking down at the little warmonger.

"Not me. I'm drawing a tank."

"I can see that. And you've done a lovely job. But that's not the assignment for today. Didn't you hear the directions?" She glanced around the classroom. "All of the other students are drawing their homes."

"I like tanks," Neal said. "Why can't I draw what I like?"

"Usually, you can," Connie explained patiently. "But this is a special cooperative project. When we're all done, we're going to post the pictures of our homes on a classroom bulletin board. It will be a fun display for parents to see at Open House."

"Then how come you're not drawing your own home?" Neal asked.

Connie looked at him, looked at the rest of the children busily drawing their colorful pictures, and suddenly she started to cry.

Marla's tiny fire escape provided a breathtaking view of Pacific Heights, the mansions, dizzying hills, pure blue sky above and water down below. But Zachary only had eyes for Marla.

"We've got to stop meeting like this," he joked, helping her to put her hands on the metal railing and caressing her body from behind with his own.

"With Connie here—" Marla started.

"I know, I know. You have to get creative. That's okay," Zachary murmured. "I like creative."

"I'm glad you were free," Marla said softly.

"That's the benefit of dating a musician," Zachary answered. "Flexible schedule."

"Not the only benefit."

"Mmm," Zachary sighed, nuzzling against her neck. "Tell me more."

Marla reached back and stroked the sides of his legs, then gripped his ass and pulled him more firmly against her. "With you, the whole package is an attractive benefit."

"You get wrapped up in what's on the outside?"

"No," Marla said, turning around to face him. In this position, she used one hand to unzip his slacks, the other to free his straining erection. "I get wrapped up on what's on the inside."

"Inside my pants?" he teased.

She slid her flimsy skirt up to her waist in front, pushed aside the lacy thong to reveal her bare naked sex and waited for him to enter her. As soon as he did, she said, "Not inside your pants, inside my body."

After that, there was no more speaking. They moved together, the rumbling of traffic wafting up to them, the sounds of the city like a melody. Marla pushed herself up on the railing, wrapped her legs around Zachary's waist, and held on. He cradled her in his strong arms, pulling her against him and then slowly withdrawing. In and out he slid. Faster and faster, until he had met and matched the pounding rhythm of her heartbeat. He knew how to make it last, but he also knew his share about the importance of encores.

"Come for me, baby," he whispered to her. "Come hard and fast, and then let me take you there again—nice and slow."

To bring her to the final place, Zach slid one hand between their bodies, strumming his fingers against Marla's pulsing jewel. He worked her so slowly, so sweetly, that she couldn't help but give in.

As soon as she'd come the first time, Zachary pulled all the way out, repositioning his flush-cheeked sweetheart so that she was facing outward again. Staring with heat-glazed eyes at the city, she concentrated on the multitude of sensations vibrating within her. Now, Zachary lifted her gossamer-thin skirt in the back and entered her this way. He hadn't climaxed yet, was still throbbing hard as he drove inside. She was pliant, like melted wax, relaxed from her first round of pleasure.

When she came for the second time, Marla saw lights flashing in front of her eyes, heard bells ringing that took her several moments before she realized it wasn't the sound of bliss in her head—it was her phone.

"So here I am in the middle of the room, losing it. Mrs. Lake, the principal, takes my class and sends me to her office, saying I should sip some of the sherry in her bottom drawer that she keeps for medicinal purposes." As Connie spoke, she and Marla stepped onto an escalator at the mall. "I almost drained the whole bottle."

"You do look a bit flushed," Marla said.

"How on earth am I going to face those kids again tomorrow?" Connie sighed. "They must have thought I'd lost my mind. Grown-ups aren't supposed to have meltdowns like that. Especially not teachers."

"First off, the kids know that you're not superwoman. They've seen their parents in crises before, I'm sure. By this age, they understand that even adults have bad days. And second, they probably won't even remember what happened," Marla said sympathetically. "Kids have the attention spans of fleas."

"Maybe. But something else will set me off, something that I usually can deal with without a problem. I'm not in good shape, Marla. And I don't know what to do."

"At least, you're admitting it," Marla said as the women stepped off the escalator and began window-shopping. "That's the first step to getting control."

"No, you're thinking about alcoholism. Admitting you have a dream lover stalking you is the first step on the way to the loony bin."

"He's not stalking you," Marla teased. "You're the one who was trying to find him last night." She hesitated in front of a beautifully decorated window. "Did you tell the principal what happened?" Marla asked, looking longingly at the different items on display.

"Not really. How could I? I'd like to keep my job, and I think that if I mentioned being stalked by an imaginary lover, my boss might have her doubts."

"So what did you say?"

"I just started talking about my sleep problems. She was very sympathetic. Too sympathetic, actually."

"Meaning?"

"She insisted that I visit the district's psychologist. In fact, she called in a sub and made me go right then."

Marla turned away from the window and stared at Connie. "I can't imagine you talking to a shrink."

"It wasn't so bad actually." Connie started walking again and Marla had to hurry to follow her, trademark high-heels click clacking on the tile floor. "He wasn't one of those pipe-smoking psychoanalyst types. He was more like a friendly bartender."

Marla was eager to hear the juicy details. "So what happened?"

"I didn't plan on talking at first. I was just going through the motions to please my boss. But he was so gentle. I ended up telling him everything."

"About Ron?"

"Everything."

"And being seduced by the dream lover—"

"Everything."

"And what happened in the motel—"

"E-V-E-R-Y—"

"Okay, okay. It's just that I know you don't like to share personal stuff with strangers."

"I know. But Dr. Peters was just so easy to talk to. I trusted him. He made me feel as if he believed everything I was saying. After my most recent blow-up with Ron, that kind of connection was simply too comforting to pass up."

The women paused again, this time outside of an expensive shoe store. Lovely, high-heeled confections were displayed in every possible way: one shoe lay nestled in a tissue-filled bird's nest. Another was draped over a windowsill. Several were stacked one on top of the other in a skyscraper made solely of shoes.

"You ever shoplift?" Marla asked softly.

Connie shook her head vigorously, brow furrowed.

"Always the straight arrow. You and I are proof that opposites attract."

"You never did either," Connie said. "If you had, I'd have heard about it by now. There's no way you could keep a secret like that from me for ten years."

"That's right," Marla said sarcastically. "You're exactly like your dream lover. You know everything about everyone." Dragging Connie into the shoe store, she looked around for a salesclerk. When an impeccably dressed man approached, Marla pointed toward the window. "The black-and-white Bandolino's with the kitten heel. Size seven-and-a-half."

Connie and Marla sat side-by-side in the store's plush, cream-colored chairs. "So was this Dr. Peters shocked by your story?"

"I'm sure that he hears worse than what I had to tell him."

"But does he hear about dream lovers every day? I don't think so."

"He didn't think it was a dream lover. He said I was probably imagining someone I know. That I cast this person in my dream. Sort of like what you said. This was someone I created out of my own subconscious. Maybe it was someone I flirted with one time."

"You? Flirt? I don't think so. Try again, Doctor."

"That's exactly what I told him. But he insisted. Without even knowing it I could have responded to someone I met somewhere. I might have smiled at him. Or batted my eyelashes." Connie shrugged. "Look, I know that it doesn't sound like me at all. But maybe I was trying to prove to myself that I'm still attractive to men. You know, it's been a while since Ron and I—"

"Really?" Marla asked, interested.

Again, Connie shrugged. "Yeah, Marla. *You* don't know everything about everything either. So here we are, with our anniversary approaching once again and me starting to feel as attractive as a lamppost. Maybe I haven't been acting like myself lately because maybe I haven't *felt* like myself lately. Dr. Peters wants to hypnotize me to bypass my inner censor and find out what's really going on."

The salesclerk emerged with the shoes. Marla tried them on cautiously, looked them over, then shook her head. "They're not exactly right. Can you show me another pair like them? But different?"

The salesman grimaced and exited. Marla was his nightmare customer.

"If you did flirt with someone," Marla said, "wouldn't you remember who it was? I mean, I flirt all the time and I have a pretty good recollection of the reactions I've gotten from all the different men. The hunky guy at the grocery store who always opens a checkout lane just for me; and the fabulous Frenchman who cuts my hair, probably the one straight hairdresser in the city. Oh, and the adorable high school senior who delivered a pizza the other night. You should have seen him, Connie—"

"Dr. Peters said it's possible that I repressed the person's identity because of the guilt I was feeling."

"But you didn't do anything. Flirting is harmless fun."

"Doesn't matter. Guilt plays by its own rules. For you, flirting might be just an ego stroke. For me, the action would mean something far more serious. Like the fact that I'm unhappy in my marriage, which is something I hadn't even admitted to myself before all of this happened. And that sort of thing is what comes out in your subconscious, especially in dreams. Which is why I couldn't see the man's real face. Just super-imposed images of men I find attractive." She hesitated, recalling that the first of the dream lover's appearances had been that of Zachary, but Marla was too focused on shoes to notice Connie's change in attitude.

"Oh, look at those," she sighed as the salesman returned and set a new pair of shoes in front of Marla. These were cherry-red sandals with leopard-print interiors. It was as if the designer had Marla in mind when creating them. She slid into the heels like Cinderella claiming her rightful slipper. "Perfect," she cooed. The salesman boxed the shoes and walked them to the counter. Marla turned to Connie and said softly, "Now, let me demonstrate my favorite shoplifting trick."

"No!"

"Just kidding, Connie. Wow, are you tense." Marla walked to the cashier and handed over a credit card. "But what about the letter that Ron got?" she asked Connie as her friend followed her to the counter.

"Maybe the guy who flirted with me sent the letter to punish me for not responding to his advances."

"But how would he have all that information? Who would know you so well?"

"I don't know. I've tried to think of someone, anyone, and it makes me dizzy. I just go around in circles, getting no closer to the answer."

"Where does it leave you?" Marla pressed on.

"With that hypnosis thing."

"Can I watch?" Marla begged.

"I'm not doing it."

"You have to," Marla was vehement. "This might be the only way you can get to the bottom of all this. Explain everything to Ron. Have the doctor do the explaining for you, if you want."

"I don't want to be put in a trance."

"He won't make you bark or act like a chicken, or anything."

"You love weird stuff, Marla. You always have. But I don't."

"You said you trusted this doctor guy."

"Yeah—"

"Connie, it might be the only way to solve the mystery."

"I don't know—"

"Do it," Marla said.

"Do it," Zach said.

"Do what, baby?"

"That's not at all what someone in a trance would say," he scolded, a serious expression on his handsome face. "A person under a trance wouldn't ask questions, but would simply obey. That's the whole point of having a sex slave. The obeying part."

"That's right. I'm sorry. I am under your spell, Doctor Roberts. I will do anything you tell me."

"I like the way you say that," Zachary told her, threading his fingertips through her curly hair. "Say that again."

"Anything," Marla purred. "Anything you tell me."

"And I am telling you." He ran his hands over her face, grasping her chin and tilting her head upward. "I'm telling you exactly what I want you to do. So, now, do it—"

She parted her berry-glossed lips and took the purplish tip of his erection into the heavenly heat of her mouth. "Like this?" she murmured her words slightly slurred around his member.

"Oh, yeah." Zachary sighed. "That's right."

"Or this?" Marla murmured, bringing her hands into the action. She stroked him gently, gracefully. Her fingertips were as light and smooth as the finest-quality satin. Man, she knew how to work him and now Zachary was the one to appear as if he were in the trance. His green eyes grew glazed with pleasure and he lay back against the plush pillows covering Marla's bed. Marla bobbed her head up and down, working at a steady pace. And then, when she sensed Zachary was getting closer, she slowed the rhythm, swirling her tongue in circles to touch the most sensitive part of his sex.

It turned her on to please him. Making Zach a happy man always had a positive effect on her own libido. Sometimes, she did things simply because she knew what his reaction would be. Like meeting him backstage after one of his shows wearing only her leopard-print raincoat. Flashing him while he put his guitar away, so that he had no choice. He just had to drag her back to the tiny dressing room and have his way with her, pressed up against a cracked concrete wall and driving hard. Or giving him head in the car while they drove to rehearsal, knowing that he'd be forced to pull over as soon as he found a safe, secluded spot. Hurrying her out of the car and spreading her out against the trunk. Lifting her tiny snakeskin skirt and plunging inside of her.

Tonight had been a carefully choreographed scenario that excited her as much as it aroused him. Of course, she didn't have to be hypnotized to make Zach happy. She loved making him feel good with her body and her mind and her mouth. It took all three to make an evening work. But playing out a fantasy that she'd been hypnotized to be his fantasy sex slave only added to the pleasure. They'd started at the beginning, with him commanding her to undress, to take all of her clothes off and let him look at her body naked. Then he'd insisted that she model for him, walking around her apartment in only high heels, showing off her fabulous ass, her curvy hips, her lush breasts.

Finally, he'd decided that she should pleasure him with her mouth. Yet she wasn't ready to stop with a simple blowjob. She wanted to make the night last for both of them. So even though he'd told her exactly what he wanted, she changed the rules.

"You like this?" she asked again, bestowing the sweetest kisses in a line from the base of his body to the swollen head of his hard-on. "Or..." she started, swiveling her lithe body into the perfect position for a sensual sixty-nine. "...This?"

# CHAPTER ELEVEN

Already deep in a hypnotic trance, Connie sat stiffly in a high-backed green leather chair. A polished wooden table stood in front of her. Dr. Peters, a pleasant-looking psychologist in his mid-fifties, relaxed in his chair behind the table. His bubbly blonde assistant, Wendy, sat by a computer on Connie's other side.

"She went under so fast," Wendy said, astounded. "I've never seen anyone so suggestible."

"There's magic in these babies." Dr. Peters wiggled his fingers. Wendy giggled softly as Dr. Peters faced Connie and assumed a serious, yet gentle, tone. "Are you ready, Ms. Morris?"

"Yes," Connie responded her voice flat and void of any emotion.

Wendy tapped a computer key. The words "Digital Indentikit" flashed across the screen in pale green letters. Using the mouse, Wendy clicked on a face-shaped icon. A generic-looking head filled the screen—not too square-shaped, or round, or oval, just a simple outline of a head, the way a child might draw one.

"We'll start with the shape of his face," Wendy instructed.

In a monotone that sounded nothing like her normal voice, Connie said, "That's too round." In response to this instruction, and following additional comments from Connie, Wendy used the device to alter the shape of the head. "Too oval. The jaws are too square. Yes," she finally said, "more like that."

As Wendy worked, Connie responded to scores of possible facial features: eyes, noses, ears, lips, and hair types. She selected the ones that most resembled the image of the man in her head. Gradually, a recognizable visage filled the computer screen. The face was handsome. Stunning, even.

"That's him," Connie murmured. "That's the man in my dreams."

"Are you sure?" Dr. Peters asked coming around the side of the table. He was obviously pleased that his client had reached this level so quickly.

"He's the man of my dreams, too," Wendy snorted, not impressed at all. "It's a picture of George Clooney."

"Really?" Dr. Peters asked. "I never watch *Law and Order*."

"*ER*. And you're way out of it," Wendy sighed. "He's been off the show forever."

"All right," Dr. Peters said, returning his attention to Connie. "Let's try again. Don't worry, Ms. Morris," he said to the still-entranced Connie. "This often takes several attempts. People's subconscious's are filled with so much garbage."

Following another series of probing questions, a different face emerged on the screen. Not a movie star this time or a model from a paperback cover, but attractive nonetheless. This was the face that had flickered before Connie's eyes during the shape-shifting games of her dream lover.

"What's his name?" Dr. Peters asked softly.

"I don't know."

"Have you seen him before? In real life?"

"I don't remember."

"There's an amazingly strong repression here," Dr. Peters said to Wendy.

"Or maybe she *really* doesn't know the guy. Maybe this is just a made-up face, another fantasy of hers. Maybe it's some actor on a soap opera, or somebody she once saw at the grocery store."

"We'll see what happens when she wakes up. Print a copy, please."

Wendy hit a key. The printer on a stand across the room purred smoothly into action. Wendy crossed the room to watch the image appear.

"All right, Ms. Morris," Dr. Peters said, "I'll wake you now on the count of three. When you come out of the trance, you will feel relaxed and at ease. All of your tension will have left your body, and you will be as satisfied as if you've just experienced a wonderful massage. One, two, three."

Connie smiled. Her expression softened from vague tension to one of comfort.

"How do you feel?" the doctor asked her.

"Fine," she said. "Great, even."

Wendy approached holding the print out. "Here's your mystery man, Ms. Morris. And he's amazing-looking—"

"But I don't recognize him at all," Connie said, confused. She'd desperately wanted to be able to identify the stranger in her head.

"A fellow teacher maybe?"

"No."

"Someone who lives on your block?"

"No. I don't think so. I'm not close with any of our neighbors."

"How about where you shop?" Wendy asked. "The check-out guy at the market, maybe. Or behind the fish counter?"

"Uh uh."

"A friend of your husband's? Or one of his acquaintances from work."

Connie shook her head sadly. "I'm sorry. I've never seen him before. And you went to all that trouble. I should be able to do my part and recognize who he is." On the verge of tears, she buried her face in her hands. Dr. Peters touched her shoulder reassuringly. "It's all right."

"But I ought to know him, don't you think? I feel like an idiot."

"Don't. It could be someone you saw just once and maybe at a distance. You might not even know his name. The face could even be a composite of several people." Dr. Peters removed the picture from Connie's hands and stapled an ivory-colored business card to the corner. He handed the picture back to her. "Take this home. Look at it from time to time. Maybe something will pop into your head, jarring your memory."

"Show it to your friends," Wendy suggested. "Don't tell them why. Maybe someone else will recognize him and be able to help solve the mystery."

Connie nodded, indicating that she'd try it. Dr. Peters smiled warmly. "Let's make an appointment for the end of the week. But if you feel like you need to talk before then, call me. Day or night."

Marla liked to do it outside. Away from the bedroom, the apartment, the fire escape, the normal places even adventurous couples might play. Now that Connie was staying with her, she had to be more ingenious in her sexual outlook. But that was no problem for Marla. She was known for having sex on the brain—dressing for it, daydreaming about it, planning for an event when something took hold of her. Today, she was feeling a bit of an exhibitionist. The thrill of potentially getting caught turned her on like nothing else. This was why she'd had Zachary meet her at work.

"I don't get it," he said, looking around at the frilly dresses on the racks and the crocheted sweaters draped over the mannequins. The floral skirts, rhinestone-studded high-heels, sequined handbags. "You don't want me to buy you something here, do you? I mean, you own the place—"

It was funny because Marla had created this idea only after Zach had taken her on stage at the club. He'd made love to her at his workspace and now she wanted to return the favor. Still, she didn't expect him to understand right away. That wouldn't have been fun at all. She wanted him to experience the element of surprise. Patiently, she took his hand and led her beau into the front window. She'd spent hours doing the display, setting up for prom season, and the whole time she'd had this idea at the forefront of her mind. Wouldn't it be amazing? Could they get away with it? Now, she'd see how closely connected she and Zach really were. Would he read in her eyes what she wanted him to do?

"It looks great," he said, glancing around. Marla had chosen a mint-theme for this window. An old-fashioned changing station was set up, with a semi-sheer green curtain over a rod. Draped over this, were several fantasy-inducing undergarments: stockings, bra, ruffled panties. The other side of the window held a leopard print fainting couch that Marla had borrowed from a second-hand store down the street.

Now, as Zach watched, Marla stepped behind the dressing curtain and began to peel off her clothes. "Oh, man—" her boyfriend sighed, sitting down on the couch. "You're not serious."

In answer, Marla began to place her own ruffled undergarments over the edge of the curtain, hanging up there with the rest of the finery. First, a lace-trimmed camisole with pearl buttons that ran down the front. Next, a pair of the most adorable lilac polka-dotted panties with frilled edges.

"Someone will see," Zach insisted, looking out at the darkened street. The Haight was never entirely empty. In fact, it was often busier at night than during the day.

"You're right," Marla said, peeking out at him. Now, she'd gotten down to a pair of gray garters and fishnet stockings, shiny high-heeled black leather boots, and a cut-out bra that revealed rather than concealed most of her ripe, round breasts. "But here's the thing," she said as she moved into the window, fully on display now, "We're in San Francisco, baby. Nobody is going to care."

Zach turned to glance out at the street.

"Just pretend that we're a couple of mannequins on display. Someone might catch a movement, and turn to stare, trying to figure out what just happened in their peripheral vision. But so what? We'll have plenty of time to dress ourselves if some righteous busybody calls the police." She hesitated again, preparing to drive home her point. "But why would they? Because they saw someone making love? This is the Haight, the center of love, Zach. The start of the summer of love."

Smiling, Zach took his lady in his arms and kissed her in return.

Connie entered Marla's darkened apartment. She turned on a light, then dropped her stuff on the floor and headed into the kitchen. On the refrigerator, a crimson heart-shaped Post-In note read: "Home late. Don't wait up. Hope things went well with the shrink. Love, M."

Sighing, Connie crumpled the note and threw it away. She'd been hoping to talk to Marla, to discuss everything that had happened at the appointment with the doctor. But they'd have to do it later. Now her stomach rumbled and she began to search for something for dinner from the fridge. As she ate leftover Chinese food, she studied the face on the printout.

Passersby on their way to the Violet Vixen Movie House caught blurs of erotic action in the window of Elegant Desires. A stocking-clad leg thrust up in the air, a curtain of red curly hair falling forward. But nobody stopped to see what was going on. In fact, just as Marla had predicted, nobody paid the window the slightest bit of attention. Not as Zach bent Marla over and drove inside of her. Not even when their two distinct silhouettes merged into one behind the dressing screen curtain.

"Too good," Marla whispered as Zach probed within her. "Oh, yes, baby. That's just right."

She gripped onto the iron railing of the old-fashioned dressing curtain, holding herself steady. Through the sheer fabric, she could see the lights of the street, the movement of pedestrians on their way to coffee houses or clubs, to the Club Divine, her favorite bar around the corner. And all she could think about was coming.

When Zachary stopped for a moment, and bent to pick up a feathered fan displayed on a table next to the dressing curtain, Marla squealed in delight and anticipation. Didn't Zach always know how to up the ante? She'd been the one to stage this show, but he wasn't going to let her have all the fun. He took the delicate object in one fist and dragged it lightly along Marla's naked back. She shuddered all over and whispered, "Again."

"No, no," Zachary crooned to her. "Not there." Now, he brought the feather-tipped fan down lower, tickling her beautiful ass with the colorful feathers. Up and down, the feathers rippled. The sensation was intense. It sent shudders through Marla's entire body. She couldn't keep herself still.

"Please," she whispered.

"Tell me where you want the fan."

"You know where."

"So say it—"

Later, in the tub, Connie stared at the picture, propped up on the sink. Who was he? Why couldn't she make her mind focus? Each time she gazed at the picture, her thoughts wandered back to what it had been like to be with him. She knew that wasn't helping her situation, but she couldn't keep the visions away. Oh, it had been nice. Not simply the way he'd read her mind, but the way he'd made her feel—attractive, desirable. Even now, with her life in shambles, she recognized that this whole experience had changed her. But still, she needed to solve the mystery in order to get on with her life, and her mind wasn't helping.

Disappointed with herself, she dried off, then settled herself on the sofa bed and studied the picture further with no luck at all. Finally, she placed it on the table, switched off the light, and closed her eyes.

Immediately, she found herself back in the circle of light. Waiting for her was the dream lover. As he'd appeared in her first vision, his face was concealed in shadow. The bed, jukebox, candles, and other romantic furnishings were gone. It was as if she'd arrived at an apartment after the tenants had moved out and the cleaning crew had scoured the place clean.

"Hello, Connie."

"You—" she gasped. "You've come back."

"Who'd you expect to find here? Ron? Haven't you been waiting for me? Calling for me?"

"But you didn't answer. Not any of the times I tried to reach you."

"Sometimes I'll pay you a visit. Sometimes I won't. But I'll always be nearby. You can count on that."

"Do you know what you've done?" she asked him.

"I've made myself irresistible to you. You haven't come like that in years, have you? Not since you were with your college boyfriend. The jerk-off wasn't all that great in the emotional department, but oh could he ever f—"

"You've messed up my whole life. You know that, don't you?"

"What are you talking about? You look perfectly fine to me. Better than fine, really. Hot, actually. I love the way that Marla's been dressing you lately. Those sexy animal prints are really wild." He mock-growled at her. "In fact, I wouldn't mind playing out our time at the motel again. That first night was so intense, breaking you out of your tight little shell."

He moved forward, and as he approached, Connie once again knew what it would be like to let go. But she shook her head. "Keep away from me. I can't be with you right now. At least, not until you tell me who you are. I need to know why this all has happened. Why you chose me."

"I thought we got over that mental hurdle of yours. Who I am just doesn't matter."

"It does to me. Please. Tell me your name. Tell me how you found me."

"You're so persistent." He took her in his arms, held her, and stroked her silky hair. Connie once again found herself falling under his spell. Could he still read what she was thinking? Would he know what she wanted?

"Give in, Connie," the man whispered. "Let yourself go. See it in your mind, and I can make it happen."

In a flash, as she'd somehow known it would, the scene changed. Connie looked around, and instantly she placed the picture. They were at the Griffith Observatory in Los Angeles, high up in the Hollywood Hills. Lights from the city twinkled magically below. A cool air rushed over her, and she looked down to see that she was dressed only in a thin, white nightgown. The luminous fabric rustled in the breeze, but Connie wasn't cold. Her skin felt warm all over, warmer yet as the man pushed her up against the marble railing and lifted the gown in back. She felt him press into her, felt the way her body immediately responded.

Connie had always loved the observatory. Every time she visited LA, she would drive out to see it, picturing the way the place had looked in the fifties when it was used as a setting for the finale in *Rebel Without a Cause*. She understood as she gazed at the light show before her, that they were back in this fantasy place—back fifty years in the past. The Los Angeles sky was cleaner, clearer, and the stars glittered from above.

"That's right," the man said, his voice low, "squeeze me back."

Connie's body followed his instructions without any thoughts getting in the way. She was as relaxed as she'd been in the psychiatrist's office. Her movements felt languid and slow. The pleasure, as it throbbed through her body, was as easy as sweet molasses.

"It's beautiful," Connie sighed, breathing the scent of orange blossoms that wafted in from one of the valley's many orchards.

"*You're* beautiful," the man said, his fingers roaming, touching her all over.

Sighing, she did as he'd commanded. She let herself go.

When they returned to the mind set, the couple sprawled out on the softest white rug Connie could possibly imagine. The light now possessed a twinkling quality, as if the air were filled with fireflies. Connie felt incredibly relaxed, and she stared at the man with the gaze of someone truly satisfied.

"Now," she said, "Now tell me—"

"You're so focused," he said, and he gave a low chuckle, as if he couldn't believe it. "Unfortunately, your persistence poses a real problem for me." He looked deeply into her eyes. When she stared back, she saw the face represented in the picture. "I know all about Dr. Peters and your little hypnotizing session." As he held her face in his hands, Connie shivered. "Now, I must erase your memory of me. When you wake up, you won't recall playing hide-and-seek, or our fun in the motel, or our delightful days back home."

"But what about everything with Ron? He knows I was at the Creekside—"

"You and Ron will just have to try and make sense of that amongst yourselves. He'll insist you cheated, and you'll insist that you didn't. Christ, he'll be able to give you a polygraph, which you'll pass, because you won't know what on earth he's talking about."

Closing her eyes, Connie thought.

"You're right. The computer print-out could be a reminder of our little adventure."

"I didn't think of that."

"Connie, when will you realize that you can't lie to me? The games are over."

While Connie watched, the man pulled out a copy of the picture from the psychologist's office and held it in one hand. In his other, a fancy silver lighter magically appeared and a blue-gold flame shot into view. He held the picture over the flame until the paper crisped and crackled into black ash.

In real life, Connie sleepwalked into the kitchen, took a pack of matches from above the stove, and touched it to the computer printout. The paper burst immediately into flames.

Back in the circle of light, the dream lover gently caressed her. "Well done, baby. Now, listen carefully and stay still for me as I erase your memory. I know you can be a good girl when you want to. Try real hard for me now. If your brain becomes agitated, I might accidentally destroy more than I mean to. I wouldn't want you to lose any precious memories of your childhood."

"Please—" she said again, but this time, the word had a completely different meaning than it had before.

The man grasped Connie's wrists firmly. At the same moment,

Marla entered the apartment and saw Connie holding the flaming picture.

"Oh, my God, Con. What are you doing?" Marla ran forward and grabbed her friend by the shoulders. Connie struggled to free herself from two different sources—the man in her head and Marla in real life. When Marla saw that Connie was hysterical, she slapped her and got her to drop the picture. Then she stamped on it until the flames died out.

"You could have burned down the place!"

Waking with a start, Connie cried out. "He was here, Marla. He made me do it!"

"Who was?" Marla demanded, looking around the empty apartment. "What is going on?" But Connie was babbling, crumpling down on her knees and sobbing. Picking up the smoldering paper, Marla saw the psychologist's card still attached.

Leaving Connie's side, she rushed to the phone and frantically dialed a number. "I need to talk to Dr. Peters. Yes, it's an emergency!"

Connie and Marla waited outside the front door of the medical clinic. Connie continued to sob quietly while Marla stood with one arm tight around her. "It's going to be okay, kiddo. I promise. We're going to get to the bottom of this together. Don't worry. I won't let anyone hurt you."

As the women watched, the psychologist pulled up in front of the building and hurried toward them from his car. Although this was the same easy-going psychiatrist who had possessed such a calm attitude previously with Connie, he didn't look happy as he unlocked the door and led the women into the building. In fact, his whole persona seemed different, negative, even older.

Inside the waiting room, Dr. Peters spoke to Connie brusquely, entirely ignoring Marla. "Wait here until I call you. I need to get my notes together." He headed down the hallway to the office in the rear, flicking lights on as he walked.

"This is the friendly bartender-type shrink you told me about?" Marla asked as she settled herself into one of Dr. Peters' waiting room seats. "I guess you like different bars than I do." Unable to help herself, Marla shut her eyes.

"Don't fall asleep," Connie insisted. "He'll get you!"

Marla opened one eye and looked up at Connie. "I'm not afraid of your dream lover. In fact, I'd like to give him a piece of my mind. He nearly burned down my apartment. Just think how much it would have cost to replace all of my shoes."

She closed both eyes.

"Marla, don't leave me alone. I couldn't stand that right now."

Reluctantly, Marla shook herself awake. "We'd better find me some coffee then. Turbo coffee. Extra-strength."

The duo wandered down the hall to a vending machine. From the lobby, Dr. Peters impatiently called out to them. "All right, ladies. Let's deal with this so we can all go back home to our beds."

Connie and Marla returned, carrying their paper cups of coffee. Dr. Peters curtly motioned for Connie to follow him into his office. Although Marla tried to enter as well, he rudely closed the door in Marla's face. Inside the office, the doctor retreated to the chair behind his desk. "So, tell me, what's the problem?"

At his anger, Connie lost all of her confidence in the man. She mumbled incoherently. "I...he... He made me burn it."

"I can't help you if you don't at least make an effort to communicate clearly."

"The man—the man I told you about. He came back."

"What man?"

"The man in my dreams."

"I'm just not following you, Ms. Morris."

"The man we talked about."

"We?"

"You and me. And Wendy. You hypnotized me and created a computer image to help me try to place his face." She gestured toward the large desktop monitor sitting on the table nearby.

Dr. Peters looked at Connie as if she were crazy. Slowly, he opened a file on his desk. "I didn't hypnotize you, Ms. Morris."

"But you did."

Studying a paper in the folder, he said, "You complained about your life-long battle with insomnia. I suggested that you try an over-the-counter medication. Maybe take off work for a few days. Even go to a stress-management seminar. But there was no hypnosis."

"That's wrong," Connie insisted, growing upset again.

The psychologist shrugged and pushed his file across the desk to her. "Read my notes for yourself."

Instead of looking at the folder, Connie stared directly into the psychologist's face. She saw that the corner of one of his eyes was twitching nervously.

"What the matter with your eye?"

"Nothing."

"It's twitching. It wasn't doing that before."

"Look, Ms. Morris. My eye has absolutely nothing to do with you or your insomnia."

"I don't have insomnia. Call your assistant. She was here. She'll remember me."

"She'll corroborate exactly what I'm telling you. In fact, she typed these notes herself."

Connie suddenly realized what had happened. "My god," she said, "he got to you before he came after me." Frightened, she stood and hurried to the door, then turned to face the doctor. "He's done something to your brain. Erased it somehow. I'm sorry. It was my fault. Forgive me."

It was so obvious that Connie meant what she said, that her

words managed to touch Dr. Peters, softening his stern exterior. "Connie, you need help. I'm going to ask your friend out there —"

"No. You leave Marla out of this." Connie sprinted from the room and down the hall. Marla was sleeping comfortably in the lobby, sprawled on two chairs pushed together. Without waking her Connie left the building, quietly shutting the glass door behind her before running out into the empty parking lot.

In pouring rain, Connie trudged down the side of the road. She was so tired that when she saw a bus stop, she sat down for a moment and gave in to her exhaustion. Even though the bus stop had been outfitted with uncomfortable seats as a politically correct method of dissuading the homeless from camping in the shelter, Connie found a way to sleep. Her eyes closed, and instantly her dream lover was there, talking to her.

"It will be over so quickly, Connie. And then you won't be scared anymore —"

With every ounce of remaining strength, Connie shook herself awake and moved on. She walked through the storm without feeling the cold on her skin. As if in a dream, she headed for the only location she could think of. It was a long walk, but finally, she arrived at home. She stood outside her front door for several minutes before ringing the bell. When nobody responded, she turned to walk away. At this moment, Ron opened the door. Connie stared at him. There was an awkward silence. Ron was obviously shocked by her haggard appearance.

"I thought you might come back," he said.

"I need help."

He spoke in the same unfriendly tone that the therapist had used. "You have to tell me the truth in order for me to help you."

"I did before," Connie said, anguished. "I really did. Why can't you believe me?"

"Why?" he asked. "I'll tell you why, Connie. It's simple. I can't believe you because I don't believe in fairy tales." Shaking his head, Ron slowly began to close the door.

"Do you want me to make something up?" Connie shrieked at him before the door shut. "To confess that I went out and cheated on you while you were out of town? Will that satisfy you, even if it's a lie?"

"Don't worry," he sneered. "I'll find out what's really going on."

"What does that mean?" Connie begged.

Ron answered by slamming the door.


"You're unbelievably cruel," Deleen said, standing in the doorway and gazing at Ron with her startling ice blue eyes.

"She's a liar. I don't need that in my life. I don't accept it in my work, why should I accept lies from my wife."

"How about you? If she's a liar, what does that make you?"

"Come on, baby," Ron smiled, knowing from the gleam in Deleen's bright eyes that she was testing him. She wasn't really angry at all. "This is the real fairy tale: true love. Love breaks all rules, doesn't it?"

"You can be amazingly sexy when you're a cold-hearted bastard," Deleen grinned. "As long as you're never that way to me."

"No," Ron whispered back, moving close to his lover and slowly undoing the belt of her translucent white robe. "No, sweetheart. I could never be cold to you." She looked stunning with the fabric pushed open, and he trailed one hand down the line of her body, lingering at her breasts, then moving lower and lower. Deleen sighed and pressed herself against him so that he was cradling her body on the fulcrum of one hand. She rocked her body firmly, gaining the pleasure that she craved.

Ron loved how she moved, how she tilted her head back, closed her eyes and groaned. When he could wait no longer, he took one of her hands and placed it directly on the bulge of his crotch.

"See that? That's all warm-blooded American male testosterone. And it's got your name written on it."

"Really?" Deleen asked, opening her eyes wide and moving away from his probing fingertips. With a sexy wink, she sank to her knees on the hard wooden floor in the entryway. "Does it?" her fingers found his zipper and she undid his slacks and reached inside. "Let me see that close-up," she murmured just before her warm mouth met his skin. "I want to read it for myself."

Connie walked past a run-down mini mall containing a Chinese take-out restaurant, a shoe repair shop, a chiropractor's office, an antique store, and Madame Largo's Psychic Studio. All of the shops were closed, but Madame Largo's garish neon sign flashed on and off, creating a dreamy reflection in the puddles on the concrete walkway. Connie looked hard at the sign, then started to shuffle on her way. But after a moment, she realized that she had no place to go. She couldn't return to Marla's apartment, because she didn't want to put her friend in danger. She couldn't go to a hotel, because she had no way to pay.

Sadly, she leaned against a drugstore's plate glass window, then slid down to sit on the sidewalk beneath an awning. A few feet away, in a recessed doorway, a homeless man slept peacefully, unaware of the rain. Nearby his shopping cart stood filled with the man's worldly possessions. Connie realized that at this point, he had more than she did. Deeply depressed, she turned to look at different items on display in the drugstore window: a hair coloring kit, cheap watches, baby toys, and a poster promoting "Sta-Alert Caffeine Gum."

Connie's eyes shut, and her dream lover's voice boomed forward. "I'm here, baby. You don't have to run. Come back to me. It won't hurt...."

Frantically, Connie woke up, looking around. She searched on the ground for something to use, then picked up a broken piece of wood. She considered this for a moment, discarded it, and looked around some more. Finally, she looked back at the homeless man's shopping cart. Would that work? It would have to. Quietly, she moved to the cart, tugged on it, and discovered that the homeless man had used an old shirt to tether the cart to himself. Connie slowly untied the shirt, careful not to wake the cart's owner. She wheeled the shopping cart silently back to the window and then rammed the glass. A big crash sounded as shards of glass flew everywhere. The burglar alarm went off, and the homeless man leaped up.

Before he could speak, Connie pushed the cart back in his direction, grabbed the package of caffeine-rich gum from the wreckage of the window and fled. In the distance, a police alarm sounded, the howls getting closer.

Connie raced down the street, breathing hard. She swerved behind a tree as a cop car sped past. Then she waited, heart racing, but nothing happened. Slowly, she unwrapped a stick of gum, slid it into her mouth, and chewed.

# CHAPTER TWELVE

Morning found an extremely disheveled Connie standing in front of Madame Largo's Psychic Studio. In daylight, the place appeared even more lackluster than it had during the night. The neon sign in the shape of an open palm blinked on and off. Tiny colored Christmas lights were strung in the shape of a crystal ball on a stand. Who in their right mind would go for this crap? Connie wondered. But then, she wasn't necessarily in her right mind anymore, was she?

After looking around to make sure no one was watching her, she walked over to the door and pushed it open. A small chime tinkled, alerting the proprietor to her presence. Hesitantly, Connie stepped forward, blinking rapidly in the semi-darkness. She found herself in a small room lit only by several red bulbs hanging in paper lanterns. This "lobby" was filled with standard psychic items: a mandala poster, a print of a Rousseau "dream" painting, a blow-up of the hanging man Tarot card, and several dusty copies of *Psychic World* magazine. Strands of colorful glass beads served as a door to an inner room. A sign on the wall read: "First consultation: $20."

Connie made a face, both at the things around her and at the scent of cheap incense wafting through the room. This was crazy. Turning to leave, she was confronted magically by the appearance of Madame Largo, an aging psychic whose black hair color obviously came from a bottle. The woman had on more than enough makeup and plenty of costume jewelry. To Connie, she looked like one of her first grade-students playing dress-up.

"I am Madame Largo," the woman said in a heavily accented voice.

"I am Judy," Connie said, stuttering over the fake name.

Madame Largo ignored the obvious lie, but didn't say anything else.

"I'm so sorry I disturbed you. This was a mistake. I shouldn't waste your time."

"You came because you're in trouble," the psychic said.

"I don't believe in palmistry, or astrology, or any of that stuff. No offense intended. But this isn't the place for me."

"It is acceptable if you don't believe," Madame Largo said patiently. "Your faith is not necessary right now. Only your presence is important."

*And my money*, Connie thought.

"You've come for a reason," Madame Largo said, prompting her.

"My best friend is a strong believer," Connie said, still in her apologetic mode. "She's waiting for the flying saucers to land and for Elvis to come out of his hiding place."

Using a ring-heavy hand, Madame Largo gestured for Connie to follow her into the back room. But Connie didn't move. "I need to go."

"You might learn something here. There are more things in the universe than you know." Connie wasn't convinced. She opened the front door, but Madame Largo moved quickly to her side and placed a hand on Connie's shoulder. "Come, Judy."

Madame Largo took Connie's hand, as a mother would take a child's, and led her to the back room. The space was lit by an array of flickering electric candles. Madame Largo sat on a worn-out wicker chair and motioned for Connie to sit opposite her on a round, cushioned ottoman.

She turned Connie's hand upward, revealing the palm. Connie pulled back.

"I have a real problem."

By rote, Madame Largo delivered the opening words of her often-performed patter. "Problems are possibilities. Tell me your problem and I can help you find the answers."

Connie was so weary that she couldn't resist the invitation. "There was a man."

Madame Largo nodded knowingly. So many of the stories that she heard from her clients began with that sentence.

"He came to me in a dream." Too tired to try and edit her experiences, Connie explained the entire situation to the psychic, and the old woman was jarred out of her perfunctory performance. Now, she really listened. "He hid his face. I tried to resist. He pursued me. I gave in. Then he left. I thought that it was only a dream. But still it was so real. And it *was* real. He told my husband. My husband threw me out. And when I tried to find the man, he attacked a psychiatrist I'd consulted. Now, I have no place to go. And worse than that, I can't go to sleep. I just can't." Embarrassed that she must sound crazy, Connie rose from her seat. "I have to leave. I've wasted enough of your time."

"Wait," the psychic said, her accent mysteriously gone. "I can't help you myself, hon. But there is someone. Someone I know. He will believe your story, and he will be able to help you. I promise." Madame Largo looked around the room, her eyes admitting the fakery of all the decorations. "He's real, this man. His talents are pure."

Connie shook her head, skeptically, but the psychic held her fast.

"Years ago, I was so depressed that I went to a sporting goods shop to buy a gun. I told the clerk it was for self-protection, that I was frightened of living alone, but I was thinking: In an hour I'll use this thing to kill myself. Then, as the clerk wrote up the bill of sale, a voice said, 'Don't buy it.' I looked around to see who was talking but no one was near me."

"Maybe you imagined...."

"I know the sound of my thoughts. This was a man talking to me. He said, 'Go to the park across the street and wait for me there.' I didn't even give the clerk an excuse. I left the store without buying the gun and I went and sat on a bench, and there he was. Waiting for me as he'd promised. I talked to the man for hours, and the pain I was feeling left me. I must have seen him, but I have no picture of him at all in my memory. It's like it was all erased. All I know is that he saved me."

Connie shook her head. "I'm a teacher. I can't have this in my life."

"It's in your life already. You don't have a choice."

Connie closed her eyes.

"The man told me I'd know how to reach him if I had to. I've never had to try before. But I'll do it now. For you."

"Don't."

Madame Largo entered a momentary trance.

"I don't need any imaginary helpers!"

Connie remembered the sign about the twenty-dollar consultation fee and opened her purse. She pulled out the twenty. As she did, Madame Largo looked at her with clear eyes. "Joseph will meet you this afternoon at the Bay Meadows race track."

"I'm supposed to meet an invisible man at the races?"

"He'll let you see him." Connie offered Madame Largo the twenty. The woman refused to take it. Connie shrugged and put the money back in her purse. As she started to leave the room, the psychic spoke again. "Judy, you must meet this man."

"Madame Largo, I've never gone to the races in my life. I never will. And my name isn't Judy."

"Mine isn't Madame Largo. But that doesn't matter. What's important is that you let Joseph help you."

"Not in a million years."

Connie headed toward the street. She turned to see Madame Largo mouth the words. "He will help."

"So, what do you really think happened with your wife?" Deleen asked Ron as the morning sunlight played over the mattress. Even though this was the bed her lover shared with his wife, Deleen felt comfortable and at ease. She had an inner power that seemed to radiate, making the surroundings appear as if they'd been designed just for her. "Do you think she was telling the truth?" she continued.

"What do you mean?" Ron asked.

"You always described her as such a boring person with no life outside of the classroom. Did she cheat on you for real?"

"Connie?" Ron snorted. "She's definitely lying about something, but she couldn't have cheated. She doesn't have it in her. She's the type of person who will actually give back money to a cashier if she receives too much change." He looked down at his lover, who lay semi-tangled in the sheets of his bed.

"Then what's all this about?" Deleen asked.

"You want to know what I really think? I think she made up the whole story as a desperate plea for attention. I think that is exactly something she and her pathetic friend Marla would come up with together. Checking into a motel. Writing that idiotic letter. Sending herself flowers."

"Then why won't you listen to her?"

"Easier not to," he said. "I've been waiting for an opportunity just like this since I first met you. I couldn't have created a better situation for myself if I'd tried. Now, I'll simply tell her that I'll sue her for being unfaithful and for the mental anguish she's put me through. She'll have to settle to the divorce terms that I request because she'll be too embarrassed to admit she made everything up. I won't lose my shirt in the process."

As he spoke, he pushed the sheets aside, revealing Deleen's

beautiful naked body. Although he didn't even want to admit the concept to himself, there was a sort of naughty charge about making love to his girlfriend in his marital bed. How many nights had he stayed awake, fantasizing about getting together with Deleen while Connie slept unknowingly at his side. He'd wait until he was sure Connie was solidly asleep, then go and email Deleen a sexy message. Or if she were traveling, call her in her hotel room and engage in filthy phone sex. She never minded being woken up, always seemed at the ready to describe just what she would do to him if she were at his side.

Now that she was really here, he looked down at her for a moment, trying to decide just where to begin. Sometimes, it was a bit over-whelming to be in her presence. When he and Deleen were apart, he thought about her all the time, lost himself in numerous erotic visions. Every time he jerked off, he had her a different way. Bent over his desk at work. Tied down to his bed with satin bindings. Pressed up against the steamy glass wall of a shower while he soaped her all over. But here she was, on his California King mattress, waiting for him to please her, and he experienced a second of unexpected insecurity.

Then, nodding to himself, he simply slid on top of her, as if the simplest way was the best. Parting her nether lips with the head of his erection, he introduced her to the pleasure of his morning hard-on. The intensity of the intrusion made Deleen start at first, and then she relaxed and put her hands up on his shoulders, steadying herself for a missionary-style ride. Her long cardinal-red nails grazed his naked skin, sending a shudder down his spine. He loved it when she touched him. Anyway that she touched him.

Yet rather than coo any sweet nothings as Ron moved inside of her, Deleen spoke only about the business of their relationship.

"Then it's really going to happen?" the woman sighed.

"Yes, sweetheart," Ron promised, nuzzling his stunning lover. "Of course, it is. You just have to trust me."

# BOOK THREE

*Oh, in waking, the sights are not so fair.*

—Christina Rossetti

# CHAPTER THIRTEEN

Connie moved aimlessly along the crowded walkway at Bay Meadows. She looked around occasionally, scanning the faces in the crowd as if she'd lost her companion. But how could she have? She'd never met him before. So what was she even doing here? Every time she tried to work that question out in the jumbled mess of her thoughts she came up with a simple answer: she had nowhere else to go and nobody else to turn to.

Several times it seemed as if someone said her name, but when she spun around, she could find nobody looking in her direction. Finally, the race began and Connie moved closer to the benches circling the racetrack. The track announcer called the race as the spectators roared. Connie watched for a moment then slipped into a seat next to a man who was focused intently on the Daily Racing Form. From the corner of her eye, she sized him up, startled when his outline blurred slightly in her vision. She blinked and looked again, catching sight of a black sweater, curly hair, tanned skin—

but wait. That was wrong. Straight blond hair, pale gray coat. She rubbed her eyes hard and looked again.

This was Joseph Hill, tall and dark-haired, wearing simple, nondescript clothing. He looked to be in his early thirties, with small lines crinkling at the corners of his eyes. He used the copy of the Daily Racing Form as a sketchpad, covering the margins with beautifully executed pencil portraits of fellow gamblers. Glancing over, he smiled at her. His smile was brilliant, touching not only his lips, but the depth of his eyes.

"Hello, Connie."

She stared him up and down, and even though she'd expected something eerie like this to happen, she spoke angrily. "I don't know you."

"I'm Joseph."

Now Connie looked away.

"I understand. You were taught not to talk to strangers. But Madame Largo introduced us this morning, so technically we're not strangers." Connie pressed her lips together forcefully, but her expression revealed that she was considering Joseph's words.

"No, this isn't a scam."

"I don't like any of this at all."

Joseph said nothing.

"Your little mind-reading act."

"Then stop thinking to yourself and start talking out loud. It will be easier for both of us."

"Why should I talk to you?"

Joseph shrugged and started to rise. Connie watched him stand and walk away. Then hesitatingly, she followed. He was her only hope. Who was she to let him leave? At the ticket window, Joseph stood in line with Connie at his side. She noticed that one of the sketches on his newspaper was an incredible likeness of her, capturing her simple, striking features, her worried-looking eyes, and the dark smudges of fatigue in the hollows beneath.

At the window, Joseph placed $500 in front of the cashier. "Mutual Fund, to win." The seller handed over a ticket.

"Your bet, ma'am?" the seller asked Connie. She hesitated, almost completely broke now.

"Give the man your twenty, Connie," Joseph urged quietly. "On Mutual Fund."

Like a robot, Connie took the money from her purse and handed it to the seller who gave her a ticket in exchange. Connie and Joseph headed toward the grandstand. "This is crazy," Connie said. "I think gambling is strictly for losers."

"I never gamble."

"You just gave that man five-hundred dollars."

"And in thirty minutes, he'll give me five thousand. You'll get two hundred, which you can use to treat Marla to a special dinner tonight at Lula's. As a thank you for all that she's done for you. Putting you up, and putting up with you—"

"Stop it! However you're doing that. Stop. Please."

They walked in silence past gamblers intently studying their sheets. Joseph got into line at a food stand. "Want a hot dog?"

Daring him, Connie glared into his eyes. "What do you think?"

"You'd love one, but you're calculating the fact that you have four dollars remaining in your purse and that will leave you with two-fifty if I'm lying about the horse winning." Grinning, Joseph ordered two hot dogs and gave one to Connie. She took a ravenous bite, realizing that she hadn't eaten anything since the leftover Chinese food at Marla's early the previous evening.

"How do you know your horse will come in first?"

Joseph looked around, as if he was afraid passersby would hear. "Shh."

"Well, how do you?" Connie whispered.

"Just wait, Connie. Don't be so anxious." He led Connie back to their seats.

The trumpet blared the call for the race. While waiting for the horses to enter the starting gate, Connie eavesdropped on two gamblers sitting in the row ahead of her. "I like Broken Promises. He won a week ago, without his regular jockey. With Ramon on him he can't possibly lose."

"He couldn't win with Shoemaker. Watch Down Draft put him away."

Connie leaned forward, caught in the speculation. "What do you think of Mutual Fund?"

"I wouldn't bank on him, lady," one of the men told her.

Connie sat back, demoralized. "I shouldn't have bet. I'm totally broke until payday, and I can't go back to Marla's place. I can't put her in danger any longer. God, I almost burned her house down as it is."

"Then why did you bet?"

"You made me."

"I ripped the money out of your hand?"

"No, but..."

"Think about it, Connie."

The horses took their places as the track announcer said, "The horses are in the gate. And they're off!"

People cheered. The gamblers in front of Connie and Joseph traded a pair of binoculars back and forth. The first one urged on the horses. "Promises, show your stuff!"

"Let's go, Down Draft!" the other hollered.

"And it's Mutual Fund on the outside," the announcer called out.

The crowd roared. Connie jumped up, too.

"Can I borrow your binoculars?" Connie asked one of the gamblers. The man checked her out as if deciding whether or not she was a safe bet, then handed over the glasses. "Come on, Mutual Fund," Connie pleaded. Throughout the excitement, Joseph remained seated, reading a paperback about the theft of a famous Vermeer.

At the sixteenth pole, Mutual Fund moved into the lead. The track announcer's voice hummed with energy. "It's Mutual Fund by a neck, Torpedo Baby second, and New Freeway third. And Mutual Fund wins it, Torpedo Baby second, and New Freeway holding on for third."

Connie jumped up and down. Joseph looked up at her, bored.

"How did you know?" Connie asked Joseph. He aimed the binoculars toward the track for her, focusing on the horse's head.

"Don't tell me that you read horses' minds, too?"

Joseph chuckled, then tilted the binoculars to box seats near the finish line. There, two gangsters looked extremely pleased with themselves. Connie returned the binoculars to the gambler, then faced Joseph. In a low whisper, she hissed, "You mean the race was fixed?" Joseph clasped his hand over her mouth and then led her back to the ticket window to collect the money. Connie looked happily at her winnings.

"Are we going to bet again?"

"No more sure things today. Besides, someone I know has a show opening at a North Beach art gallery. Want to join me?" Connie nodded and followed Joseph toward the exit. "You know, you could be the richest man in the world," Connie said when they arrived at Joseph's car, an ancient black MG.

"I don't want to be the richest man in the world."

"But you *could* be."

He shook his head and unlocked the door. Then he started to unlatch the convertible roof. Connie helped him lower it. "If for some reason I ever got greedy, they'd be onto me in a flash."

"They?"

"People who claim to have 'important' uses for the power. They collect people who possess it." The two climbed into the car and Joseph gunned the engine. The MG moved along, winding through the traffic and out toward the well-manicured streets of San Francisco. "I've worked hard to keep away from them."

"And me? Would they want me?"

"You're a receiver. Receivers are a dime a dozen. They need senders who can slip into the minds of foreign ambassadors or spies or soldiers or whoever they like to target."

"The guy who came into my dream? Was he a sender? You've read my mind. You know what happened."

Joseph nodded.

"Why did he come into my life if I'm no use to them? It couldn't be just for the mental sex, right?" She blushed as she said the words, but she didn't look away from Joseph.

"People have done some pretty twisted things for sex. Don't you read the papers?"

"But the letter. Why would he send my husband a letter proving that I had an affair with him—and would that even count as an affair? As cheating? Really, the whole thing was all in my mind—"

Joseph shrugged. "It all depends on where you draw your limits, right? Remember Carter, with his famous line about all the adultery he'd committed in his heart. And then Clinton, of course. Oral sex isn't really sex. So what do you think, Connie? Where are your barriers? Is it sex if you fantasize about it? Or sex if you cross the line—"

She shrugged. "I don't know. I thought I knew, but I don't know anymore. A week ago, I would have said that anything that happened in your thoughts was free. Just for you. Then this all took place, and now I'm confused."

"You've got a right to be. You haven't really slept now in too long. Sleep's essential for keeping the brain working."

"He can get me when I sleep."

"Not anymore. I can help you."

"But can you find out who the man was, and what he wanted from me? Was it just a malicious attack, or was it personal for a reason?"

Slowly, Joseph shook his head no. "You saw what happened to Dr. Peters. Going after your man would be like taking out space on the biggest Internet search engine there is. They'd find me in a heartbeat. After all the years I've spent avoiding them. Building up my barriers."

"So you won't help me?"

"Not to track him down. You're like a house with no doors. You're so open, anyone with five lousy watts of ESP could set up shop in your brain. Hell, it doesn't even take ESP to read your mind. Your husband bullies you around. Your friend Marla coerces you to do things you don't want to. Even your students lead you through hoops. I can protect you and Marla while I show you how to install an effective psychic security system. And that's about it."

"Then I'm just supposed to forget what that guy did? Let him get away with destroying my life?"

"I would."

*But what about my marriage?* Connie thought sadly. *I can never explain this so that anyone will believe it. So what about Ron? Do I forget him, too?*

As they drove on in silence, Joseph slowly nodded. Connie suddenly realized he was reading her every thought.

"Stop it!"

"When you stop your mental chattering."

"Where could she be?" Marla begged Zachary.

"Anywhere, baby. She could be anywhere. It's a big city."

"But there are only a few places Connie would feel comfortable. She couldn't have just disappeared into thin air."

"She probably went off somewhere to get her head together," Zach assured his girlfriend. "She'll come back when she's got it figured out. Connie's tough. You should have faith in her."

"This isn't like her. She should have called."

"Everyone needs some time alone, Marla."

"But she doesn't have any money. Doesn't have anyone but me to help her."

"You're not Connie's keeper," Zach said, petting Marla's hand. "You need to believe in her. She's a grown-up."

Marla shook her head, still upset. And Zach gave in.

"Would it make you feel better to go out looking again?" Gratefully, Marla nodded, and Zach handed over his second helmet and the two went outside to his waiting Harley.

Connie and Joseph entered a gallery/cafe on Lincoln. It was a large, concrete-floored room filled with cutting-edge portraits and nudes, all obviously by the same artist. The techniques in the paintings differed—some were entirely monochromatic: pure reds, clear jewel-toned blues, electric greens. Others were as detailed as photographs. But something in the pictures tied them together—an understanding of the subjects and an ability to imbue the paintings with a rich depth.

The gallery owner waved to Joseph, smiling as she walked forward. Joseph waved back casually, then steered Connie over to a wall, where they could look at several different paintings. Connie took her time studying the artwork. When the duo reached a large painting, Joseph stopped. But although she tried, Connie couldn't concentrate on it.

"What you're offering isn't enough."

"What can I tell you?"

"I don't need you. You're wrong about me. Nobody bosses me around." The words sounded false to Connie's own ears, but she continued on, heatedly, unwilling to give in to the perception that Joseph had offered. "I'm my own person. I don't even know you and you're making judgements of me." Suddenly angry, Connie turned and stormed out of the gallery. Joseph moved to another painting and scrutinized it, not even seeming to notice her absence.

But this wasn't true at all. He noticed. He saw everything. The way her face had lit up as she'd yelled at him. The way her eyes glowed with a mesmerizing intensity. She was lost in the depth of her situation, confused and desperate, and her need pulled at him. Although it had been years since he had allowed himself to even look hard at a girl, to think about what it might be like to be with someone, Connie had managed to affect him.

With his skill—or his curse—it was too difficult to get involved in a relationship. There were simply too many tempting moments to reach into someone's mind and find out what that person was thinking. Too many ways to get hurt.

With distaste, he remembered his last real relationship, discovering how Valerie had really felt about him simply by plucking her thoughts from her mind. He'd known when she was attracted to another man, when she was faking her emotions with him. Ultimately, it had destroyed anything he'd felt for her. Even though he could read within her that she truly did love him, he wasn't able to forgive her for her trespassing thoughts. Slowly, a distance had grown between them. When she came home one evening, eyes downcast, face shadowy with sadness, he'd been the one to break up with her. Knowing that it hurt her too much to say the words. Always, he was sparing other people pain—somehow not able to protect himself from that ultimate emotion.

But Connie was different. He'd sensed that from the moment he first saw her, first felt her confusion throbbing in his head. The power that he had was difficult to live with at times. It was so easy to abuse. Looking into Connie's mind had taken him only a moment, and he'd been floored by what he felt from her—the naivete of her thoughts, the desperation that she was going through.

Jaded from his years of city living, he tried to remember the last time he'd brushed up against innocence.

Marla and Zachary cruised the streets of San Francisco, taking the curves and the wild rollicking hills with a graceful ease. Zachary handled the machine the way he handled his guitar—and the way he handled Marla in bed—with a powerful combination of respect and finesse. At stoplights, Marla directed him to the different places she thought Connie might go: the wharf, their favorite coffee shops, the Palace of Fine Arts, until finally they'd been all over the city with no luck.

"Don't be so hard on yourself," Zach said to Marla when they paused by the side of the road to regroup. "Let's just go somewhere and relax for a little while. When Connie's ready to talk, she'll come home to you. I promise. Until then, there's nothing you can do to help her."

"Where do you want to go?" Marla sighed.

"I've got an idea of how to take your mind off all this—"

"You're not serious," Marla said.

"Try me."

Marla sighed as Zach drove them back to her apartment. When she slid off the back of his bike and pulled her helmet off, he said, "I promise that I'll take your mind off your worries, baby," and Marla gave him a sad little grin in return.

Connie hurried along the sidewalk in a furious haze. She passed an ice cream parlor next to the gallery without even seeing it. But after a moment, she turned around and walked back to the shop. Despite possessing zero desire for food at the moment, she entered the shop.

Standing at the counter, Connie read the menu board with glazed eyes. Then she said forcefully, "I'd like a banana split." The clerk put an oval-shaped crystal dish on the counter and began to scoop out the ice cream. "Put more ice cream on the plate." The clerk raised his eyebrows, but added more ice cream. Then he poured on the chocolate sauce. Frantically, Connie continued to make demands. "More sauce. More!"

"What do you want to do, lady? Corner the chocolate market?"

"Keep pouring. I'll pay double for it. Triple."

Other customers watched with amazement. Connie paid and carried the giant dessert to a corner table where she sat and stared at the gargantuan concoction. Looking down at the banana split, she began to cry.

Zach didn't need the handcuffs at all. He wanted them. There was a big difference in the world of bedroom play. Marla knew from many pleasurable au natural experiences in the past that he was perfectly adept at making love without toys, but the addition of extra paraphernalia added to his excitement. And this added to Marla's. Sometimes, Zach liked to use his oily black leather belt around her wrists, holding her in place. The stark quality of leather against her skin turned her on. Other times, he favored the sensuality of fur-lined leather cuffs, or the sturdiness of a pair of her own nylons. Today, he was going old school.

Naked and captured to her bed with the cold steel handcuffs around her wrists, she waited for him to join her. Zach took his time, sitting on the edge of the bed and running his fingers up and down the tender skin on the insides of her calves. This made her shiver, an odd tickling sensation that was entirely unique. He followed his fingertips with the tip of his tongue. Oh, she would melt. The feel of Zach's warm, wet tongue on her had Marla straining against the handcuffs, which was obviously exactly what Zach had hoped for.

He watched for a moment as she struggled against the metal, as she begged him with her body to take care of her. And then, he gave in.

"I can't wait any more," he sighed. "I really need to have your flavor on my tongue."

Marla couldn't have fought him if she'd wanted to, and she didn't want to. She just lay back and savored the moment as Zach brought his full lips to her delta of Venus, spread her nether lips with his fingers, and went to work. Or play. Or whatever you call it when your boyfriend goes down on you. And oh could he go down. Zach knew all the tricks, the special make-it-last tricks that you only learn after years of loving women. He pressed the flat of his tongue against Marla, firmly, until she groaned as the first flicker of sexual fire burned through her. Then he made darting circles around and around until Marla arched her hips on the bed, trying to connect more firmly with his mouth.

This was why he had chosen to use the cuffs. They gave Marla a little room for action, but mostly left Zach in charge, which was exactly how Zach liked it. Marla realized at some point that he was still dressed, while she was nude, and that made her wetter still. Zach was intent on only bringing her pleasure, in the slowest way possible stretching it out until her whole body seemed to vibrate.

But finally, he seemed to want to feel her skin with his skin. And he stood and stripped, losing his clothes quickly. Naked save for his indelible tattoos, he lay on the bed next to her. Marla wished her hands were free so that she could touch him. But Zach didn't seem to mind, getting his body next to hers, caressing Marla with his skin. He arched his back, rubbed himself on her, and worked in a way that made her think of a panther stalking along the mattress toward her.

As he moved up the bed, Marla lost herself in the feel of him, the scent of him, the warmth of his body on her own. Every time they made love, she felt as excited as she'd been on their very first encounter. His movements turned her on in an unexpected way.

She threw her head back and let the waves of pleasure rock over her, burst inside her like the surf pounding against the shore of the Bay. They shook her body from the inside out, took her away and then gently, and slowly brought her back down again, into Zach's loving arms.

Joseph gazed at another intricate painting, the same intense focus on his chiseled face. Connie entered the gallery in a slow shuffle, looking entirely demolished by the experience in the ice cream parlor. She approached Joseph and stood quietly at his side. When he didn't speak, she searched for something to say.

"You knew I'd come back."

"I can't predict the future."

"You made a total fool out of me over there. I wasn't hungry. I didn't even want any ice cream in the first place." She wasn't accusatory in her tone, simply spoke the truth in a low, unsteady voice.

Joseph said nothing. His silver-gray eyes remained focused on the painting.

"You win," Connie sighed.

Joseph faced her, a look on his face like a stern father. "It's not a game, Connie. I can't win. *You* can't win. Maybe if we're very lucky, we'll survive."

Connie stared at him. Everything she had was on the line.

Her face took on an intensity that had been lacking to this point. "I want to learn from you. I'll do whatever you say. I won't challenge you again."

"It'll take time."

"I've got plenty of that." She gave a small laugh. "In fact, it's all I've got."

"The lessons won't be easy."

"I'm not afraid. Not anymore."

Joseph stared at her, seeing deeper than anyone else could.

"Okay. I am afraid," she confessed. "A little. A lot."

"You should be. That shows you're not a moron." They moved on, pausing in front of an elegantly simple still life: pale lemons in a straw-colored basket. "You've got strength in you," Joseph said softly. But it's buried."

"How can I find it?"

"By keeping your mind clear."

# CHAPTER FOURTEEN

Connie entered Marla's apartment. Although more bedraggled than ever, she appeared somehow at peace. Joseph had done that for her. His easy-going manner and faith in his ability to protect her had crossed over to Connie. Now she was calm and relaxed-looking rather than crazed and out of control. Marla, who hadn't slept in a day, ran to Connie and looked her up and down. "You're a mess. What happened to you?"

Connie yawned and observed Marla in return. "You're no fashion plate yourself."

"How could you leave me like that? Do you know how worried I've been? I haven't slept a wink since you ran off. I've been mainlining coffee." She held up one trembling hand. "See?"

"Thank God." Connie sighed. "If you'd slept, he might have..."

"Where the hell have you been, Connie?"

"It doesn't matter."

"Don't you get it? I've been frantic. Looking everywhere. Zach has been cruising the city on his Harley, going into the worst neighborhoods looking for you. I've called hospitals, the police, even Ron. What an ass that man is."

"I'm all right. I'm better than I've been in a long time, actually." But Connie stumbled as she spoke, practically asleep on her feet. Marla grabbed her and helped her to the sofa.

"If this is good, I'd hate to see you on a bad day." She hurried off then returned with a glass and a bottle of whiskey. She poured Connie a tall drink. "Some medicine. Then you can tell me everything. Or I'll beat it out of you—" she tried to make that sound like a joke, but it was obvious to Connie just how upset Marla was.

"Were you in a hospital, Connie? Were you hurt?"

Connie smiled. "Actually, I was at the races."

That didn't make any sense to Marla. It was the last place she would have thought to put Connie. Gambling was definitely not something her friend was into. "Look, kiddo," she said. "You better tell me everything. What's been going on?"

Connie tried. She closed her eyes and did her best to formulate the story that would make the most sense for Marla, but she didn't know where to start.

"Don't edit," Marla insisted, correctly reading her expression "Just tell."

At her insistence, Connie took a sip of the whiskey and started to talk. She found that as she spoke, she really wanted to share everything. To have someone on her side, someone who would react to what she was saying and give her the straight-talking feedback that she needed to hear. She told Marla about running away from the doctor and going to see Ron. And she told her about Madame Largo and Joseph.

"It sounds like a con," Marla said, skeptically.

"I don't think it is. I know it sounds crazy, but the whole thing's been crazy. From the very beginning right up until now."

"What do you have to give him in return?" Marla asked, refilling their glasses.

Connie shrugged. "Nothing."

"Nothing?"

"He didn't say. I don't think he's like that. I think that he genuinely wants to help."

"Men don't want to help," Marla said emphatically. "They always expect something in return. If it's not money, then it's something else." She raised her eyebrows in a knowing arch, indicating precisely what she was talking about.

Connie tried to recreate the good feeling she'd had earlier in the evening with Joseph, but the alcohol was starting to dull her senses. As she took another sip of the drink, she thought that maybe Marla was right. Maybe the whole thing with Madame Largo and Joseph was some sort of intricate set-up, preying on the fragility of her mental state. She could have made herself order the ice cream, right? That wasn't so far off base. She'd always resorted to sweets when she was depressed. And Joseph could have been watching for her at the races, sitting down next to her when she wasn't paying attention. Perhaps the whole situation with the psychic and Joseph was part of an elegantly designed scam.

Marla spoke the words for her. "What if they're in it together with whoever sent that letter?"

"That just doesn't make sense," Connie said. "I found Madame Largo completely by accident. It would be too much of a coincidence to think they are in collusion with the letter-writer."

"That's exactly what they'd want you to think. And the doctor could be involved, too," Marla insisted. "He seemed a little creepy to me." She suddenly snapped her fingers together. "You know, I saw this whole thing the other night on *Mystical Mysteries*. The episode focused on different psychic and paranormal phenomenon. And one of the things the host said was that psychics crave feedback. Some of them will read about something in the newspaper or online and then work that into their shtick. This could be even bigger than you first thought, Connie."

"I don't know," Connie said sadly. "I just don't know."


Joseph sat at his easel, waiting for inspiration to come. He never forced his creativity. He respected his talents—both mental and artistic—and let things happen when they were supposed to. But although he was in the mood to paint, his canvas remained blank. Connie was on his mind, not his art. He looked over at his bed where the Racing Form lay open. There was the sketch he'd drawn of her. Maybe he'd transfer that simple line drawing to the canvas. He wouldn't even need to refer to the pencil sketch. He already knew what Connie looked like. Intimately, he knew the shape of her eyes, the form of her lips.

A slight fear pulsed through him. He knew from many past experiences that this was dangerous territory, getting involved in someone else's life, in the mess of it, in the tangled webs that would undoubtedly continue to pull him in. Now that he knew her and liked her, he'd never be fully free.


When she closed her eyes, the dream lover was there waiting for her. He took a second to appraise the way she looked. Even in this dream place, Connie was drunk. She found it difficult to stay in one place, moving slowly back and forth in front of him.

"I do like the way you act when you're a little buzzed," he said. "Slightly slurred in your speech. A little mussed around the edges. Not so uptight and teacher-like. You should kick back more often. It suits you."

"You're here," she whispered. "You're back."

"Yeah, Connie. I'm here. You knew I'd come around for you again. That's why you went to see that psychic lady. Looking for help, right? A way to find me—"

Connie waited for a moment, but the man didn't mention Joseph. She didn't offer him up and for some reason he didn't seem able to read about Joseph's existence in her mind. Instead, she sighed, too tired to fight. What use was there? Maybe she should just give in. Then she saw the glint of silver handcuffs cradled in one of his palms. After they'd discussed Connie's situation, Marla had drunkenly told her about the evening's erotic events with Zach. Connie understood in a flash that this was why the man now had the tools in his possession. An erotic charge pounded steadily within her. Could she allow herself another fantasy? Try it out for a night? She knew the feeling of those cuffs around her wrists. Understood in a mental premonition what it would be like to strain fiercely against the metal, but to be bound and unable to get free.

"My bad girl," the man said softly. "I need you to stay still for me. These will make things easier on you. You understand, don't you?" When she didn't reply, he continued. "You'll be good for me this once, Connie. Won't you, baby?"

No, she wouldn't. He was going to erase her mind, and she couldn't let him. With every bit of strength left inside her, Connie woke up, pushed herself off Marla's velvety sofa, grabbed her purse and headed out the door. Trembling all over, she squeezed her eyes tight and mentally called out for Joseph. Nothing. No response at all. Then she remembered his phone number written on the back of her Bay Meadows receipt, and she reached into her purse and dialed him on her cell phone. "I need you—"

That was all she had to say.

"I know," he said. "I'll be right there."

"I don't know what to do." Connie stood in Marla's parking lot, her arms wrapped tightly around her body. A light rain—more mist than rain—decorated her golden hair with crystalline drops. The weather made it difficult to tell whether she was crying or merely wet from the weather.

Joseph sat in his car, looking up at her. "I'm glad you called me,

Connie. Let's go upstairs and talk about it."

"I can't put Marla in any more danger. He came back. He could come back again and hurt her. Make me do something else crazy. Burn down the whole place this time."

For a moment, Joseph was silent, thinking about their options. Finally, he offered a solution. "Would you like to come to my place? Would that make you feel better?"

Now she nodded, giving him a grateful look. At her response, the feelings inside Joseph were surprising. He wanted to help her. But as Marla had expected, he wanted more. With an effort, he damped those feelings down inside. This was just him offering her a place to stay, not a sex thing, not a date thing. Simply a space on the oldest couch in the world, covered by a quilt his grandmother had made for him twelve years before. He'd had many guy friends crash out at his pad before, and one or two girls had spent the night there, as well. But still, he told himself, she was coming to his house to sleep over.

Was it wrong?

He told himself to keep it above board, to do the right thing, repeating these words in his head to make them real. So instead of getting out of the car and hugging her close to his body, which was what he really wanted to do, he reached out his hand, and she took it, needing all the support she could get to make it upright to his car.

The drive to his apartment on Hillcrest was unimpeded by traffic at the late hour, but slow anyway, due to the light rain. The water made the roads slick and dangerous, and Joseph concentrated on the drive. Neither one made any attempt at conversation. Connie rested her head against the window, and after asking her if it would be all right, Joseph turned on the radio, his favorite station, K101, oldies but goodies. He was humming along to "Goodnight, Sweetheart," when he realized that Connie had fallen asleep.

Quickly, he surveyed her state of mind. In his presence, he knew she was safe. The dreams she had were pure and peaceful—a vision of herself in a backyard hammock, rocking slowly beneath two large oak trees. He was satisfied that she'd be secure, locked away in her mind. Now that she was with him, the ESP attacker would be unable to approach.

Arriving at the apartment building, Joseph looked over at Connie, still asleep with her head leaning against the window. Instead of pulling into the covered garage, he drove around the block three times, not wanting to wake her. Each time he circled, he passed Heartbreakers, the dance club across the street from his building. You could see the red heart-shaped neon sign from one of his windows. It blinked until close to three-thirty in the morning, served as a nightlight when he padded down the hall in search of a late night snack or glass of water. Usually, throngs of people waited restlessly outside the club. Now, nearing last call on a rainy weekday night, the only person on the street was a rabid-looking bouncer, who stared fiercely at Joseph as he drove by the third time, daring him to try to start some trouble.

Joseph didn't want any trouble, not for him or for Connie. She looked so worn out. She deserved a few extra moments of sleep, and he didn't want to wake her by stopping the car and turning off the engine. But finally, after circling a third time, he pulled into the garage and eased into his parking space. Still, she didn't wake. When he opened his door, closed it gently, and went around to her side of the car, she didn't even open her eyes. After considering his options, he opened her door, lifted her into his arms, bumped the door shut behind her, and carried her into the building. She was light and easy in his arms. Again, his mind took him to places he wasn't ready to go picturing Connie with her legs around him, her eyes open and staring at him with pleasure.

He wondered what his neighbors would think if any of them got on the elevator with him. He was carrying a near-comatose girl into his apartment, after close to three years of never having any dates. Would they believe that he'd knocked her out, used that date rape drug to try and get some? He was relieved when they made it to his place without running into anyone.

"Here we are," he said, more to himself than to her. Connie murmured something unintelligible in her sleep, and pressed her head more firmly against Joseph's chest. In a gallant move, he took her down the hall and set her in his bed. He was sure the scenario wouldn't matter to her. She was so out of it. But he'd feel better knowing that she was sleeping on the best that he had to offer. He waited a moment, staring at her while she slept, before he took a pillow and that old quilt out to the living room and went to sleep out there.

Except that he couldn't sleep. He wasn't the slightest bit tired now. Restless, he turned the radio on low and sprawled out on the sofa. He propped his head against one of the tattered cushions and looked out the window at the neon-streaked night. With each flash of the sign from the club across the way, he thought about Connie, nestled in his bed, only yards away. He thought about what it would be like to lift the covers and slide under there with her, wrap one arm around her slender body and pull her close to him, protecting her from everything bad—bad husband, bad dream lover.

It was so pathetic, lying there in the dark listening to old love songs, imagining himself to be her savior. He'd have laughed out loud if he didn't feel so serious about her. And so quickly, too. He didn't believe in love at first sight, but with his mental powers, there really wasn't anything "first sight" about a meeting. He had the ability to know her most secret thoughts, to see that she had nowhere else to turn.

Was that love? This need to protect someone? He couldn't remember, but he didn't think so. Maybe it was simply lust, the thought of how soft her skin might feel against his body, the warmth of her, which he knew now from holding her in his arms. The way her mane of golden hair would tickle his chest. And how her lips would part at the moment his brushed against hers.

He stared up at the ceiling, fantasizing.

# CHAPTER FIFTEEN

"Here's the deal," Joseph said to her in the morning. "You can't half-believe. The power doesn't work that way. You have to put everything you have into this. Every single cell of your body has to be working to protect yourself or he'll be able to get to you. Give me everything you've got, Connie. That's the only way I can help you. It's 100 percent or nothing at all."

Connie nodded. She rubbed the sleep from her eyes and took stock of the apartment she was in. It was a nearly empty room with just a bed and an easel and more painting supplies than she'd ever seen outside of an art studio.

"You drank with Marla last night. That made you vulnerable to him. I was able to keep him away once I had you back here, and I was able to hide your knowledge of my presence in your mind. But when I'm not around, he can get you when your defenses are down, and I can't protect you against that sort of thing. Not drugs." He held up a hand when she started to interrupt. "Yeah, I know you're not a user. Smoked pot once in college, just to see what it was all about. Refused to do X with Marla, which pissed her off considerably. I've read it all in your head. I'm just letting you know. Not drugs of any sort. Prescription or recreational—no Xanax, no Valium, no liquor." He hesitated. "I also can't protect you from Marla and her conspiracy theories."

Connie grinned with embarrassment at that. Marla was filled with all sorts of ideas. Skeptical of what was going on with Connie, but ready to explain the situations based on what she learned from her tabloid papers. Connie had been tired enough to get sucked into her crazy way of thinking. Joseph handed over a cup of coffee and continued his lessons.

"I know you want me to help you, and I can sense that you're ready. So this is where we are. I'll protect you from this man until you are strong enough to protect yourself. And I'll teach you everything I can about gaining the strength you need. Can you handle that, Connie?"

She nodded. "I'm taking a leave of absence from school until I can get this all figured out. I'd be no good for the children right now."

"Smart thinking," Joseph said. "When you go back to work you'll be even stronger."

"But there's one thing I just don't get," Connie said earnestly. "Why is he after me? Why won't he just let it go?"

"If he's part of the organization that I think he is, he can't risk you going public with your knowledge. These people work in secrecy. That's their main weapon. They can't have the general population knowing about them. He wants to erase your memories, Connie, and he's not going to be extra-careful to keep your mind intact. He has no reason to care about you. So let's work on getting you tough enough to protect yourself. Go home and explain to Marla that you were out on a walk to get your head together. Don't tell her about me again. Pretend you believe her mumbo-jumbo. Then meet me for lunch in the Marina and we'll start."

Connie drove to the Marina and parked by the side of the road.

Across the street, she could see the Babaloo Beach Cafe. Red -and-white striped umbrellas stood at every outdoor table, shielding the beautiful patrons from the dangers of the sun. At one corner table Joseph sat alone, lost in his sketchpad. As Connie approached, his outline grew fuzzy in her vision. Was he wearing a baseball hat or an old-fashioned fisherman's cap? Jeans and a T-shirt? No, khakis and a blue denim button-up. She shook her head to try to focus, and found herself suddenly seeing him. As if for the first time, really seeing him.

"That's right," he said as she sat down. "Focus." He didn't even look up at her, simply continued drawing. But in her head, she heard his voice continue. "Listen to yourself. The inner voice will be very soft at first, almost impossible to hear. When you can hear yourself in the quiet places, try listening everywhere you go."

At first, Connie was confused. She heard the noises of those around her. One man at a nearby table made phone call after phone call on his cell. From the sounds of the one-sided conversation, Connie realized he was making multiple dates for the evening. An early drink with a girl named Wanda. Late dinner with Gloria. Dancing at midnight with Charlene.

"Your husband was right when he said that life can be like a soap opera," Joseph continued inside Connie's mind. "But you don't need to watch the other actors around you. Pay attention to yourself. Right now, you're the most important person there is."

Blushing, Connie tried again.

"You must face every part of yourself. Including your greatest fears," Joseph continued. "Work on it for a week. Then come back to me. I'll help until you're strong enough. You don't need to worry about him. Just worry about yourself."

At first, Connie didn't know where to begin. She wished Joseph had given her more to work with. Her greatest fears? Man, she was scared of just about everything. It was one reason she'd initially linked herself with Marla. The girl seemed to have no fears at all as far as Connie could tell, and she found it invigorating just to be near her. But now, Joseph was telling her that she had to change. Not superficially, either. Change from the inside out. What wasn't she afraid of? Speaking in public. She did that everyday, and some people found that more frightening than death itself. What else?

Sitting outside on Marla's fire escape, Connie made a list of her fears:

*Heights/fear of falling—that was pretty normal, right?

*Being alone—but that just came from having always had a roommate, or a husband. She just didn't have practice.

*Making people angry at her—that was huge. It was why she'd had such a difficult time standing up to Ron about even the smallest things.

*Fear of letting go—she'd begun to confront that fear with her dream lover, and look where that had gotten her.

So how could she get stronger? She closed her eyes and thought about what Joseph had said. Face your fears. Then she went inside and looked through the yellow pages. Marla wandered in from the bedroom and saw Connie rifling through the phone book.

"What are you doing?" she asked, looking over at the list.

"Chronicling my fears."

"Let's see—" Marla said, snatching up the notebook and reading the words that Connie had neatly written in her classic teacher style. Connie felt odd at having Marla look at what she'd written, but she bit her lip and waited for her friend's response. Marla read each listing, nodding to herself.

"How about you?" Connie asked. "You're not really afraid of anything, are you?"

"What are you scared of?" Zachary asked.

Marla shook her head, already trembling all over.

"It's just me. But where am I?"

Blindfolded, Marla reached her hands out, trying to touch her boyfriend. Each time her fingertips got closer, he moved away.

"What do you think I'm going to do?"

That was the big question. And this was what Marla had asked for. Asked for, yes, but maybe she hadn't bargained on how it would make her feel. Sure, they'd played bondage and dominance games before. Yet everything had been open. Carefully discussed and prepared ahead of time with safe words and all sorts of checks and balances to keep both partners on the same page. Now, Marla was truly in Zachary's power, and she had to put her trust in him, her total faith. This was the fear she was facing.

"What do you think?" he asked again? "Huh, baby?"

Suddenly, there was a flash of light, bright even beneath the heavy silk of the blindfold. She locked onto the sound immediately from past experiences. He was taking her picture. She heard the motor of a Polaroid, and then the click again. What part of her body was her photographing? Her breasts? Her ass? Her face? She couldn't be sure.

"Smile, baby," he crooned. "Let me see those beautiful lips of yours part for me. Open up." Again, the camera clicked, but Marla didn't obey her man. She was shaking all over. She could hear his voice coming from one part of the bed, and then quickly from another. And she felt oddly disoriented and unable to process everything fast enough to feel at ease in the situation.

The pictures were raining down on her. The cold backs of the instant photos chilled her skin. He was taking so many. The bed would be covered. And then suddenly he started a whole new game.

"Now, guess," he said. "Guess what I'm touching you with."

First, he used a feather. She knew that from the initial touch. A lone feather tracing up the insides of her legs. Back and forth, climbing higher until it had almost brushed that magical spot at the center of her body.

"A feather," she murmured. The sensation stopped immediately. And then, she felt something cold. What? The base of a glass? No. A candleholder? A perfume bottle?

"I'll touch you until you guess," he explained.

She thought hard about what it was, and then finally, she said, "Hairbrush."

"Good girl," he praised her.

Next, she felt something long and hard, wooden and thin. "Drumstick," she giggled. Leave it to a musician to bring a drumstick into the bed! If she'd been dating a handyman, he'd undoubtedly have brought in his tools, right?

She worked to catch up with Zach, who was already tracing a new toy along the basin of her belly. This was also long and thin, and Marla tried to figure out what it might possibly be. The spiked heel of one of her shoes?

"That's not it—" Zach said.

"What do you mean?"

"This is it—"

She heard the click of his lighter, and then felt the stunningly powerful charge of hot melting wax dripping onto her naked skin. It was just like in that sexy music video she'd seen on MTV, except here the man was decorating the woman with the wax, rather than the other way around. The pain was intense, an instant flare-up that made her want to cry out. But then Zach brought his mouth to the quickly hardening droplet, and he licked there, licked firmly, replacing that pain with an amazing pleasure. While she was basking in the experience, another fiery droplet fell on her skin, and then another. Marla realized that she'd forgotten the rules of the game. Zachary would keep taunting her with the melting candle wax until she named the device he was using.

"Wax," she said in a rush. "Hot wax."

"That's right," he said, maneuvering himself between her thighs. "So now let's go with something harder—"

Marla giggled softly. Although she didn't plan on naming the next item any time soon, she had no doubts at all what that something might be.

Connie spent over a week confronting her fears, and each day she learned more about herself. Her main fears were not necessarily rational, but they were plenty real to her. To start with, she'd always thought she had a fear of getting a massage. Stripping down in front of a stranger and feeling that person's hands on her naked body terrified her. It was why she'd always refused to go to day spas with Marla, making excuses about not having the time, or not being tense enough to need the luxury. In truth, she didn't want anyone to stare at her, to judge her, let alone touch her.

Crazy, right?

But Joseph had said to confront her deepest fears, so she booked herself an appointment at a high-end salon in San Francisco, arriving in a jittery state and trembling from the moment the sweet-faced woman behind the counter handed over a thick, terrycloth robe.

"Damon will meet you in Room Number 3," the receptionist told her. "Change in the dressing room, then just head down the hall."

She'd thought of leaving right then. Paying for the appointment and then literally running away. But she forced herself to follow the instructions of the woman behind the counter. And as soon as she found herself naked under a sheet on a leather table, felt the hands of a knowing masseur caress her shoulders, she lost that fear immediately. She wondered how many of her fears would evaporate once she took a good, hard look at them. Had she been tormenting herself for years with fears that really didn't exist?

Next up was dealing with the alone factor. She took herself to lunch, sitting at a table without any partner, without even any reading material. Focusing hard, she concentrated on how she felt, and soon she realized that she felt fine. Her own company wasn't a bad thing. Quiet wasn't a bad thing. She didn't need constant noise, constant attention. In fact, Connie learned she observed more of the world around her when she was by herself. She noticed how other people spoke to one another, how they dressed, how they interacted. Rather than dwell on what some stranger's image might be of herself, she lost her worries in a newfound interest in her own surroundings.

But finally, she found that she had to deal with the more serious fears—the ones that caused a ripple of panic to course through her. Fears she thought she'd never have to confront. The fear that maybe her entire marriage had been a mistake—

No, she wasn't ready for that one yet. She'd try a different one first.

Deleen pushed through the clothes in Connie's closet, searching for something alluring. There wasn't much to choose from. Connie's tastes ran toward the prudish. But Deleen didn't give up. She pushed onward until she found the closest thing to a sexy nightgown that existed within the whitewashed space. "What about this?" she asked Ron, modeling the beige lace number.

"Take that off."

"Don't be like that."

"Now," he insisted. "Take it off now."

"Come on, won't you play with me?"

"Play how?"

"I'll be Connie and you be you. I'd like to see how you deal with her. Haven't you ever tried role-playing before?"

"Why do you have this need to dwell on my wife?"

"I'm just interested," Deleen said, pulling the nightie over her head and becoming herself once again. Naked and extremely confident in her own radiating beauty. "Don't you ever want to know what my husband's like?"

Ron shook his head. "I know what your *next* husband is like," he said, stepping forward and taking Deleen around the waist. "That's plenty good enough for me."


Under the watchful eye of a jump instructor, half a dozen student jumpers prepared to leave the plane. The first five went. Connie was next. She looked down, got dizzy from the sight of the earth so far down below, and stepped away from the door. The jump instructor came close to her and placed a hand firmly against her back.
"Need a push?"

Connie angrily faced the woman. "No, I don't need a push. I don't want a push." She moved to the door, closed her eyes for a second, opened them, and leaped from the plane, freefalling her way down to a fearlessness she'd only dreamed about.

# CHAPTER SIXTEEN

At an upscale restaurant in the heart of SOMA, a small jazz combo played softly. The music was cleverly designed not to intrude on the dinner conversation, creating a careful ambiance of tasteful romance. Joseph entered the room. The maitre d' led him to a table where Connie sat reading the menu. Her hair was up in an unusual fashion for her. It wasn't just a simple ponytail, but twirls of golden strands framed her face, highlighting her lovely cheekbones, her startling green eyes. With Marla helping her to dress, she had started to develop her own style. This evening, she was wearing a violet dress that hugged her figure, a lavender velvet wrap, and a slender gold chain around her neck.

Other patrons checked her out as they walked by. Connie exuded a newfound confidence. She was drinking mineral water with a slice of lemon—no wine, no whiskey.

"Joseph," she said, staring at the menu. "The prices here are unbelievable."

"Lucky for us we had Gold's Fool in the third. Twenty to one."

The waiter hurried over. The couple consulted with him then placed their orders. After the waiter left, Joseph gave Connie a gift-wrapped package the size of a large book.

"It's a day late, but happy birthday."

Connie grinned. "How did you—" Then she stopped, realizing exactly how he knew. Smiling, she pulled off the colorful wrapping paper, revealing a small oil painting. The artwork stunned her. "It's beautiful," she sighed. "I'm not just saying that—"

"I know."

Connie laughed. "You painted it."

"The signature gave you a hint?"

"Thank you," she said to him. "I'll treasure this forever."

The food arrived and they started to eat. Across the room, a sour-faced man began to verbally abuse his sad-eyed dinner partner. For a moment, the other diners all grew still with the discomfort of the situation. When the man signaled for the check, he suddenly knocked his full glass of red wine into his companion's glass, dousing himself. The crash and his shouts drew everyone's attention.

"How did that happen?" Connie asked.

Joseph, his expression serious, said nothing, but she heard his voice in her mind.

"You?" she whispered.

Joseph shrugged. "His wife should leave him before he grows violent. But unfortunately she won't."

"You said you don't predict the future."

"That's not a mental prediction. I can tell just by looking at her."

Connie nodded, drinking in Joseph's sad expression. Then she smiled and took his hand. "Dance?"

"I don't know how to dance to this sort of music."

"I'll teach you."

Slowly, the couple approached the tiny dance floor. When the band members saw Connie and Joseph heading in their direction, they switched to a dance tune. Connie faced Joseph.

"Ok, now put your..."

Joseph eyed the band guys who were watching them intently. There were no other dancers on the floor. Embarrassed, he said, "Don't say it. Just think it."

Connie laughed, delighted. This was the first time since they'd met that she knew more about a subject than Joseph did. Her face showed concentration as she and Joseph began to dance. At first, he was awkward and seemed miserable. Without knowing what he was doing, he stepped on her foot.

"Ouch! You're supposed to come forward when..."

Joseph gave her a nasty look. "If you visualize it, I'll get it."

She pressed a finger to her lips and closed her eyes the better to mentally see the dance moves. Joseph took her in his arms again, and as he moved, he began to improve. His movements became smoother.

"Ready for something tricky?" Connie whispered.

"No."

Her expression was intense. She was obviously determined to have her way.

"I said 'no.'"

Connie grinned. In spite of himself Joseph executed the complex dance move with her, spinning Connie as the music ended, then dipping her deeply. The two looked into each other's eyes, reading each other's minds, with Joseph better at the game than Connie. But she understood anyway. She saw what he wanted her to see, and maybe a little more than that. An image flashed quickly in her mind— she and Joseph entwined his arms around her. Connie flushed, and Joseph had to work hard not to drop her. What was going on?

Without speaking, they returned to their seats, both a bit breathless from the exchange but unwilling to discuss it. The waiter returned, pushing the dessert cart.

"Would you like to try one of our fantasy confections?"

Connie glanced at Joseph, still blushing. Yes, she would. Something totally a fantasy, and totally a confection. But not made in any pastry kitchen. Joseph felt her leg brush his under the table.

"What do you have to offer?" he asked, ignoring her touch.

The waiter began to identify the different selections. "Fresh raspberries with creme fraiche, chocolate decadence, amaretto mousse, orange-sherry cake and the chef's specialty: creme brulee."

"Everything looks delicious," Joseph said.

"I'll pass."

Joseph looked at Connie, then eyed the cart, eyebrows raised.

"Really," she said. "I've had enough." Joseph stared at her and furrowed his brow, as if firing powerful psychic beams at her.

"Joe, stop it."

The waiter looked at the couple, puzzled. Joseph started to laugh. "Just coffee," he told the waiter. "Two. Black."

"Where you really trying to get me to order dessert?" Connie asked after the waiter pushed away the cart.

"I really was."

Connie was elated. "I've made progress, Joe."

"I can tell."

"Today something amazing happened. I stopped by my school to pick up some paperwork I'd forgotten. The substitute was in the middle of a science lesson, facing the board, and my back was turned from the class as I rummaged through my desk. I heard—if that's the right word—one of the kids thinking to himself that he was going to pour water onto another kid. And I didn't even turn around. I just said, 'Peter, water isn't for throwing.' The kid was totally shocked, and when I realized what had happened, I was shocked, too."

Connie smiled at Joseph. "He wasn't trying to enter my mind, but I was able to enter his. That's like being a sender, isn't it?"

Joseph didn't like the direction Connie was headed in. "Sort of," he said, looking around for the waiter with the coffee.

"Don't you see what this means? I can go out and find the guy who seduced me and make him tell me why he did it. I can prove to Ron that I didn't actually cheat."

"Is that so important? To prove yourself to Ron?"

Connie shrugged. "I don't need him back. But I need him to know what happened. I need him to know that I just had fantasy sex. If I work hard enough, I can fix everything."

Joseph shook his head. "That would take more strength than you have, Connie."

"But today...at school."

"You were able to do it with a child who was only a few feet away, but you must see that that's different from searching the country—maybe the world—for someone who's a definite pro. He'll have defenses you can't possibly imagine."

"How do you know I don't have the ability to do it?"

"I know."

"Prove it."

"You want me to give you a test?"

Connie nodded.

"Get our waiter to bring us that coffee right now."

Connie turned and began to raise her hand to signal the waiter. Joseph reached for her wrist and pulled her hand back down. "Not like that," he said, still holding onto her arm. "Send a mental command for him to bring us the coffee."

Connie looked at Joseph, pursed her lips, and tried to send an order with her thoughts. The waiter, who was talking with a scantily clad woman at the bar, didn't even turn their way. Joseph smiled satisfied he'd proven his point. "Given up?"

Making a face, Connie said, "I'll try again." This time she closed her eyes and concentrated as hard as she could. But when she opened her eyes again, the waiter had moved on, busy helping another table.

"Let me give it a whirl," Joseph said softly. He rubbed his forehead melodramatically the way Madame Largo might. Suddenly, the waiter hurried toward their table, silver coffeepot in hand.

"He was going to come anyway."

As she spoke, Joseph rubbed his temples again. The waiter stopped for no reason at all. Standing like a statue in the middle of the room.

"All right," Connie sighed. "I get it."

The waiter, released by Joseph, arrived at the table. He poured more coffee, placed the bill face down, and departed.

"So you can do it better than I can," Connie whispered. "But together, we'd have no trouble locating the man and forcing him—"

"We'd have plenty of trouble. More than I want. More than you would want if you could just understand what I'm telling you. I can protect you here, but if you go gallivanting who knows where—"

Connie was upset. "I hoped, when you started teaching me, that you'd change your mind once I showed you that I could learn."

"I knew what you were hoping," Joseph said, matter-of-factly. "It would have been impossible for me not to know."

"But you still won't help me?"

"I can't."

"I'm going to do it anyway. I don't need your help. I'll find another teacher." As Connie stood from the table, she looked down at Joseph. "What kind of friend are you, anyway?"

Joseph just shrugged.

"You're afraid. That's all. You're not sure you're a match for whoever's behind this. Maybe you think you'd lose."

"Maybe you're right."

Connie walked away from the table. Calmly, Joseph sipped his coffee. After a minute, Connie returned and picked up the painting she'd left under the chair.

"Don't think you forced me back here."

"I wasn't thinking that at all."

"It's just that I like the painting," Connie explained.

"I'm glad that you do."

They exchanged a long look.

"I'm not afraid anymore," Connie said softly.

"Sometimes fear can be a friend," Joseph told her.

"I don't know. That just doesn't sound right—"

"Come back to my place," Joseph said. "And we'll talk some more."

# CHAPTER SEVENTEEN

The dream lover looked everywhere for Connie. Searched her out with no luck. He couldn't understand how she'd disappeared. Maybe she wasn't drinking, wasn't making herself vulnerable to him, but was she really not even sleeping? He knew that there were uppers to keep people awake, pills more serious than the non-prescription types, but at some point she'd have to give in. It wouldn't be possible to stay awake for days—to go this long without crashing.

He paced in the circle of light, his anger building until the room transformed from a golden-hued romantic setting to one lit in a bright red glow. There was nothing erotic here any more—no bed, no flowers, no pretty love songs. There was only his anger, growing, enlarging until it pulsed in a hot halo all around him. He didn't call out to her as she had to him. There was no use in that. Instead, he sat down on a steel-backed chair that appeared at the moment he wanted it. With all of his mental strength, he focused on alleviating his displeasure.

If he couldn't play with Connie, that was fine with him. He'd play with Ron instead.

It was all about rules, power and rules. No matter who your partner was, there were rules to games like this. Ron knew them. He'd explained them to other lovers plenty of times—lithe young girls tied down with silk scarves or bound with leather thongs and silver handcuffs, or simply held down, their trembling limbs captured in his strong hands. Deleen wasn't the first lover he'd had since getting married—not by far.

*If you want to stop, at any time, just give me your safe word and I'll stop*, he'd tell them. They rarely needed to, because he never pushed that hard. He liked to take them as close to the brink as he could without ever going over. It was a way for him to test himself, to see if he could read a person's wants and needs to make their fantasies come true in dark and exciting ways.

But Deleen was different this evening. It had been her idea to play a little bondage game, and she didn't seem to care about the rules, didn't seem to know they existed. She looked like she might take him over the edge, and he didn't even have a word to give. Deleen suddenly kissed him, sending his mind spinning. The pleasure that roared through his body was enough to silence his questioning mind, still his troubled nerves. But when she backed up and looked down at him again, all the fears came rushing back. Ron didn't know what to do. He'd never played submissive before. And although he'd witnessed his share of scenarios at Sinsation, a high-end bondage club in town, and although had seen plenty of subs in action on his own, he just didn't know the drill. Everything in his head told him to fight. Not to play the way Deleen wanted to, not to give in to her. When the lights were on, it had been easier. With the lights on, he could feel at least in control of where he was, could get a grip of the situation. In the dark, he felt thrown off balance.

"Hard for you, isn't it, baby?" Deleen murmured, her voice sounding soft and understanding. She was right next to him, on the bed with him, and a tiny bit of light from the hallway came into the room and flickered over her face. A look in her eyes made him nod that yes, it was hard to do, and his nod was rewarded instantly with a harsh slap. It had been a trick question. Ron swallowed over the sound of pain and surprise, biting down on his bottom lip instead of letting out the sound.

"You answer me with a verbal response. I don't like 'Ma'am' or 'Mistress,' simply 'Yes, Deleen' will do fine."

He didn't say anything, wasn't sure what she wanted from him. Still in her steady, calm voice, she repeated the question, "It's hard for you, isn't it, Ron?"

Now he tried to make his mouth work, make the correct sounds come out. It seemed very important that her answer her correctly. "Yes, Deleen," he whispered.

"Louder."

"Yes, Deleen," he said, his voice more normal sounding in tone, which pleased him. At least he could hide a bit of his fear. He tried to be rational with himself. This was a game—a kinky sex game. He'd played kinkier. So he'd never been tied down before. Nothing huge there. So why was he scared? What was it about the way his girlfriend was looking at him that made him feel as if he'd been thrown down a dark pit?

"We haven't even started yet, Ron," she told him, now making him feel like a little kid, the way she said his name. Taunting him. He tried not to analyze each step of the dance, but couldn't help it. Deleen stood up and walked across the room. He heard the sound of a match, and then he saw the candles. She lit one after another, mesmerizing him with the light.

Sitting back on his chair, the dream lover smiled.

When they got back to Joseph's apartment, Connie tried to make Joseph see her side. "I thought you liked me, Joseph. I thought you'd see how important this was to me and that you'd help."

Tears streamed down her face and Joseph wished he could think of something to say that would comfort her. Connie sat on his sofa next to him, her shoes off, bare feet curled under her body. With her arms wrapped around her slender body, she looked small and vulnerable, like a child waking up from a bad dream. It seemed like days rather than hours since they'd had dinner together, joking over the food and wine. Dancing, even.

Her body shook with silent sobs and she turned her head away from him. He hated himself for being the one to make her cry. Even though he knew it wasn't really about him. It was about the man—

"I really thought you did," Connie said again, sounding even more melancholy. She looked miserable.

He wanted to say, "There, there, it will all be okay," the way his grandmother had comforted him when he was upset as a child. "It's not about how I feel," he said instead, handing her a box of Kleenex.

"Then what is it?" Connie took a tissue in her hands and Joseph watched as she shredded it, watched the snowfall of Kleenex bits flutter to the floor. His puppy thought it was a game and went flouncing after each little piece, chasing and killing it before it hit the ground. Joseph grabbed the little guy and barricaded him in the bathroom.

Joseph sat back down on the edge of his sofa, facing Connie. He put out one hand, to brush away her tears, but she shook him away. "Finding your own way is the most important thing right now. Searching out that man isn't what you need."

"How do you know what I need?" She spoke louder now, and

although her voice had lost the anger, the emotion was still there, pulsing right under the surface. "You might be able to see my thoughts, but that doesn't mean you know what's deep inside." She buried her face in her hands, "I thought you'd help. I thought you liked me, Joseph," she said again.

Oh, God, he was going to have to tell her.

"I like you, Connie. I like you a lot."

He stood up and started pacing, and Connie, still sobbing, fled the apartment.

*My luck*, he thought, shaking his head. *Just my luck*.

# CHAPTER EIGHTEEN

"Shut the shades," Marla said softly.

"Why, baby?"

"We don't want to shock the neighbors—"

"Oh, forget about that," Zach said. "You're going to move in with me soon, anyway. These neighbors won't even be on your mental radar screen any longer. Let's give them a final show to remember."

Despite her initial hesitation, Marla liked the sound of what Zachary was suggesting, and she stood and made her way to the window. She had to walk slowly, because she was wearing a pair of decadently high-heeled shoes, ones she'd bought from the store right next to Elegant Desires. It was a store she'd always felt catered to strippers. Maybe they did. The shoes were insane in their height, but oh did they make Marla's legs look amazing.

"You look good in those," Zach said, watching her move.

"How good?" Marla asked, holding an erotic pose and waiting for his response. Zachary spoke with actions rather than words. He moved forward, running his hands down her body, coming to rest on the curves of her haughty ass. He cupped her here and brought her forward so that she could feel the power of his sex. But then, when she thought he would slide aside her lemon-yellow thong and get down to business, he surprised her. Going on his knees, he pressed his tongue against the tiny diamond of fabric covering her delta of Venus and he kissed her there.

"Good enough to eat," Zachary murmured into her skin.

"I like the sound of that," Marla responded softly as Zachary continued to lick her against the lace. The barrier between his mouth and her sex made the sensation even more intense. She could feel the heat and the wetness without getting the contact that she absolutely craved. The denial was an aphrodisiac, making her wetter by the second. Marla could just imagine how good it would feel when Zachary finally slid aside the little fluff of fabric and pressed his warm mouth directly against her skin. But until he did so, she leaned back on the windowsill, parted her legs, and enjoyed the ride.

"I'm playing tonight," Zachary reminded her, and his words vibrated against her skin, sending a delicious tremor all the way through her body.

"I know."

"I mean, playing on stage. Not just playing you—"

"I know," Marla laughed.

"You going to come see me?"

It was getting more difficult for Marla to talk. Each time Zachary spoke, his words worked against her in the most delicious manner. But Marla knew that as long as she kept up her end of the conversation, so would he.

"Do you really want me out in the audience?"

"Of course," Zach said against her skin. "I like to sing all my songs to you."

"Maybe me and Connie will come—"

"I don't know about Connie," Zachary said, deftly sliding aside the lace and letting Marla finally feel his naked mouth against her skin. "But I'm pretty sure you're going to be coming...and soon."

Zach's Harley wasn't in the space when Connie parked. She was infinitely relieved to see that, wanting to be alone with her friend. No, she couldn't share everything she'd experienced with Joseph, but Connie knew that just being near Marla would help her feel better.

Still crying, Connie hurried into Marla's building. She wiped at her face with her hands to get rid of the tears, but they wouldn't stop. When she entered the room, Marla was watching the TV. A commercial played on the screen, but Marla had the sound on mute. She looked up at Connie's ravaged expression.

"Hey, are you okay?"

Connie shrugged. Wasn't it obvious that she was far from okay?

"Where have you been?"

Connie shrugged again. She didn't want to bother explaining everything to Marla, not when she knew what Marla's response would be. More conspiracy theories that just didn't add up. Instead, she said, "Long day. Just one long day."

"This show will cheer you up," Marla promised, unmuting the sound. The television showed a montage of tabloid-style video clips: a flying saucer landing in a school yard, a tightrope walker falling to his death, a helicopter crashing into a building, two pretty women mud wrestling. "TAB TV is on the air," a fast-talking announcer stated.

The words "TAB TV" flashed on and off in bright, cobalt blue neon.

"Are you really watching this?" Connie asked Marla.

"No," Marla said sarcastically. "I just turned it on to give my set something to do."

"Come on, Marla."

"This is my favorite show. Of course, I'm going to watch it. I'm psyched that it's on now, before Zach's performance. I've got to leave in about an hour."

"But this is trash."

"Sure it is. But it's good trash. Don't you ever read *Cosmo*?" *Cosmopolitan* magazine was Marla's Bible. "The latest issue explained just how important it is to zone out and enjoy some mind candy every once in awhile. Treat yourself to a mental vacation. Besides, everyone's watching this. It's the hottest new show. It'll make you forget all of your problems."

"What problems?" Connie asked. Now, she was the one who was being sarcastic.

The TV announcer interrupted their conversation. "And now the host of TAB TV, the incomparable Lyle Patterson." On the TV, the studio audience applauded excitedly as Lyle Patterson's face filled the screen. He was about forty-years-old and intense-looking, with a shtick of treating every subject as if it were the most important thing in the world.

"God, he's handsome," Marla sighed.

"Are you serious?" Connie stared at the host. Silver-haired, strong-jawed. "Striking... maybe. But handsome?"

"It's just that he's so passionate. I mean, the way he stares into the camera. It's as if he's staring right at me."

Connie snorted.

Lyle started to talk, and Marla held her hand up to silence her friend. "In show business, the words 'astounding' and 'unbelievable' are overused. But I can think of no words that better fit today's first story, which we're calling 'Love at First Bite.' Stay tuned."

A commercial came on. Maria muted the television, jumped up, and headed to the kitchen. "Want some pudding?"

"No, thank you."

Connie unwrapped the painting Joseph had given her and stared at it.

Marla returned carrying two cups of pudding. She handed one to Connie, who put it on the table. "It's chocolate," Marla said, shocked as she unmuted the set.

Before the show returned a toll-free phone number filled the television screen: 1-888-AMAZING. The announcer's voice explained, "If you've had an amazing experience, call the number on our screen."

Connie's lips moved slowly as she silently repeated the number with the announcer: 1-888-AMAZING. Connie smiled to herself. Marla turned to see her and nodded her head as if to say, "I told you this would cheer you up."

Marla parked in the lot between Savoire Faire and The Down and Out. The place held good memories for her. Savoire Faire was where she'd first caught sight of Zachary, his guitar leaning against the wall behind him. She'd liked the way he looked, and the way the guitar case looked—emblazoned with stickers from around the world—but mostly she'd liked the way he looked at her.

She had been there with Connie, who noticed Marla staring at Zachary, and advised her to play it cool.

"Don't look at him so much," she said. "Let him look at you."

But for once Marla couldn't help it. Rarely, did she let go of her tough-chick attitude, making the men work to catch her attention. But Zachary was different. Marla was mesmerized from the moment she set eyes on him.

Your average guy might have sent a glass of wine, or simply winked and motioned for Marla to join him, but not Zachary. He had the buxom blonde waitress, who'd been at the restaurant for twenty years, bring over a large pepperoni, onion, and black olive pizza. "Compliments of the gentleman in the back booth," the waitress said, "He wants you girls to know that you're way too skinny."

That was the beginning.

Tonight, his band was playing next door, and she slid into The Down and Out after giving her name to the man at the door, who checked her off the list. Zachary's band had just taken the stage, and Marla moved through the crowd until she was as close to the front of the room as she could get.

The audience was rowdy, responding wildly as Dirty White Pants did their trick of taking off their matching white pants at the end of the show and throwing them to the ladies in the crowd. One particular girl screamed the loudest, catching Marla's eye. The girl stood near the stage in a gold sequined halter-top and jeans so tight Marla wondered how she could breathe.

The little slut, Marla thought dramatically. It was an unfair assessment since she had similar outfits in her own closet.

Marla watched as the female fan reached for Zachary's pants. Her attractive boyfriend seemed unaware of the fact that girls wanted him. He made jokes about it occasionally, the macho jokes that all the band members seemed to indulge in, but he didn't seem to notice the predatory look in some fans' eyes. A devoted boyfriend, he threw his slacks at Marla, and she caught them amidst disappointed squeals from teenyboppers all around. Marla tried not to gloat, simply folded them up and smiled at Zachary, reminding herself that she got his pants all the time. The other girls simply saw a few minutes of him and rest of the band wearing their colorful boxers.

After the show, she met Zachary backstage and slipped into his lap. He cradled her in his strong arms, rocked her back and forth as if she weighed nothing at all. He was still wearing only his shirt and boxers, and Marla could feel that he was excited. That aroused her even more.

"What do you need, baby doll?" Zachary crooned softly.

"I need you."

"Where?"

"You know where—"

He did, of course. They'd done this before. Zach lifted her up and led her by the hand to the dressing room, nodding to the rest of his bandmates that he was not to be disturbed. Marla's heart throbbed in her chest as Zach shut the tiny door behind them, and slid her up against the wall. He wasn't going to undress her. That would take too long. Right now, he simply slipped her dress up to her waist and pulled down her panties. Marla loved the feeling of urgency that pulsed through them. Yeah, a long slow session could be amazing. But a quick ride in a nearly public place floored her like nothing else.

"You saw her, didn't you?" Zach asked as he entered her.

"The kid who wanted your pants?"

"You didn't think 'kid,' though, did you?"

"Slut," Marla admitted.

"You don't have to worry, sweetheart," Zachary murmured, lifting her off the ground and pinning her against the wall as he continued the ride. "My pants belong to you."

# BOOK FOUR

*I heard a noise and wished for sight,*
*I looked for life and did a shadow see.*

—Anonymous

# CHAPTER NINETEEN

Connie sat alone at San Francisco's International Airport. A small leopard-print travel bag, borrowed from Marla's overwhelming collection of interesting luggage, rested on the black vinyl seat at her side. The departure sign at the gate read: Flight 22, Nonstop Service to New York (Kennedy). 11:15. Joseph approached Connie from behind. She'd been following his lessons and his advice and her powers had grown since their last meeting. She didn't even have to turn around to know he was there.

"Hello, Joe."

Joseph smiled, pleased with her progress.

"I've missed you," Connie said, moving her luggage onto the floor so that Joseph could sit down at her side.

"I missed you, too."

Connie looked hard at Joseph. She could sense that there was something else he wanted to tell her, a continuation of a thought, but she couldn't figure out what it was. Automatically, she tried to focus her energy on feeling him out, yet wound up only with the picture of a tall brick wall in her mind—a joke from Joseph for trying to pick his brain. If he didn't want her to know what he was thinking, then she wouldn't be able to.

"So what do you think of my plan?" she asked finally.

"Dumb. Just plain dumb."

"That's positive," Connie said, "But do you think it'll work?"

"Maybe your man doesn't even watch television."

"But if he does, or if someone tells him about it, what do you think he'll do?"

"I told you before," Joseph said. "I'm no fortune teller."

The flight dispatcher picked up a microphone. "In a moment, we'll be boarding Flight 22, nonstop service to New York's Kennedy Airport." As the woman spoke, Joseph noticed a man sitting on the other side of the waiting area. The man, about fifty years old, looked bored. Connie didn't see Joseph's interest shift from her. "At this time, we'd like to offer early boarding to those traveling with small children or needing extra assistance."

Connie faced Joseph. "I'm sorry I walked out on you like that. I was being selfish. There's no reason for you to put yourself in danger. Not after all you've done to keep away from these predators."

Joseph didn't comment.

The flight dispatcher continued, "Passengers holding tickets for rows 25 through 37 may now board the flight."

"You did a good job with me, Joseph. I can't thank you enough."

Joseph smiled.

"Passengers holding tickets for rows 18 through 37 may now board."

"You were right to make me do this by myself."

"You don't get it, Connie. I'm not making you do anything. If I had any influence over you, you wouldn't even be going."

"I'll be all right. Don't worry about me."

"Who's worrying?"

Connie hugged him. Over her shoulder, Joseph caught the eye of the man, now looking in their direction. "They're about to call your row."

"All passengers holding tickets for Flight 22 may now board."

Again, she had the feeling he wanted to tell her something, something important, but she could get no clear idea what it was. Now, when she tried to see into his head, all the visual she received was a "Do Not Enter" sign. Joseph gently kissed Connie's cheek then bent and lifted her bag for her.

"I knew you were going to do that," Connie said to Joseph.

"How?"

Connie grinned. "ESP isn't the only way to know something, you know?"

She stepped back from his embrace and headed into the jetway. Joseph turned and slowly walked toward the stranger. The man appeared to be deeply engrossed in a newspaper. Joseph sat down in the empty black leather seat at his side.

"Take any nice photos, Dick?"

The man looked up from his paper. His expression showed a combination of surprise and annoyance. "Are you talking to me?"

"Did your mother know you were going to be a private eye when she named you 'Dick'?"

The man stood suddenly. Joseph looked at him hard, and slowly he sat back into his seat. "I want the film."

Stuttering, Dick held his ground. "I don't know what you're talking about."

"I'm talking about the photos that you just took for Ron Morris. The film, please—" he held out his hand.

Dick looked away, as if hoping that Joseph might just disappear.

"I know all about you, Dick. Bad for you if people hear about your involvement in the Drayton deal."

Dick faced Joseph and opened his mouth. But before he could

speak, Joseph interrupted. "Doesn't matter how I know, or who told me. You should really be interested only in who I will or won't tell. And that depends entirely on your own behavior in the next five seconds. Do I need to count out loud for you?"

The two men sat in silence, staring straight ahead. Then Dick removed a miniature camera from his pocket, opened it, and handed the cartridge to Joseph.

"Thank you," Joseph said graciously. "And if you don't mind, I'll take the roll that you shot of Marla and her boyfriend, as well the other night. We don't need those pictures to appear on the Internet, now do we?"

Again, Dick reached into his pocket and handed over a tiny cartridge.

"Now, do me a favor. Tell Mr. Ronald Morris that he's making a fool of himself by having his wife followed. Tell him that you've discovered that Connie is a thoroughly honest woman and that you feel dirty for having tailed her in the first place."

Dick nodded.

"Tell him that love isn't about facts. It's about trust. Can you remember all that, Dick?"

The private detective nodded.

"Good, then when you're done saying it, you will indignantly return the two thousand dollar retainer he gave you."

Dick gasped. "But I need the money." Joseph locked onto the man's eyes. "Look, I don't know who you are, or how you know so much about me, but you must also know that. I mean, this may sound like bull. But I'm telling the truth."

"I know you are," Joseph said. "Probably for the first time in your life."

"Please—" Dick begged.

Joseph thought for a moment, then bent to whisper something in Dick's ear. Dick glanced up at Joseph shocked. "To win?" he asked.

Joseph nodded forcefully.

"Are you sure?"

Again, Joseph nodded.

"I really appreciate this, man," Dick said.

"Hold on for a second. If you should ever meet me again, which I hope won't happen, you won't recognize me. So let's try a quick test here, shall we? How old am I?"

"I don't know."

"How tall am I?"

"I don't know."

"Show me the indignant look you'll give Ron when you quit the case and return your fee."

Dick looked indignant and Joseph smiled. "Goodbye, Dick."

Tripping over himself to get away, Dick left the area quickly. Joseph stared through the gate that Connie had walked through. His stare moved to the TV monitor listing departures.

# CHAPTER TWENTY

Marla sat at a table at the Sleeping Buddha on Market, perusing the different delicacies listed on the menu. After a moment, she checked her watch and frowned. An attractive waiter hurried to her side. "Can I get you something while you wait, Miss?"

Smiling up at him, Marla ordered her favorite drink. Then she remembered Connie's warning, and even though she thought the whole thing was nuts, she shook her head. "Wait a sec. Make that a virgin."

"Wish it were that easy," the waiter teased. "Regain your virginity in a snap." But he left for the bar, and Marla went back to studying the menu. She felt eyes on her and looked up to see the waiter staring at her admiringly. Behind him was Zachary entering the restaurant. He looked uncomfortable as he glanced around. The place was a bit high-end for this Texas-born cowboy.

"Zach."

He saw her and moved to the table, almost reluctantly. As he sat, Marla leaned forward for a kiss. Zachary avoided her lips. Marla immediately realized something was wrong, and she gave him an inquisitive look.

"Baby, I have some bad news."

"How bad?"

He studied her as if afraid it would hurt too much to say.

"Tell me. Come on."

"I'm going back to Austin."

"For the weekend?"

He shook his head. "For good—"

Marla was rocked. But like a champion boxer who's been hit, she didn't want to show the pain. "I thought things were going so well."

"Yeah," he nodded and reached for her hand, but she pulled away. "With you and me, definitely. But the music scene's just not working out for me here. I get gigs here and there, and they barely pay the beer tab. I've got an offer for a real job back home. Playing at a dive, but playing there each week. It would be regular money and a chance to build up some interest in the band. I need to take it. And I know you're not going to leave your store and come with me. You love living in the city."

"So it's over?"

He shrugged. "I can't ask you to wait for me. And I can't ask you to move."

Marla bit her bottom lip. It was obvious what she was thinking. No mind reading necessary. "This doesn't have anything to do with you. This doesn't always happen to you. You don't pick the wrong guys. Nothing like that. You're going to be fine."

She took a sip of her drink, which turned into a hearty swallow. "I'm sorry," Zach said gently.

"No big deal," she said. Zachary sat opposite her, staring. "We had fun, right? So go. Just go." She forced a smile. Zachary stood up and moved away. In the corner of the room, he found the waiter and offered money for Marla's drink. Then he tried a smile that was as false as hers and left.

The waiter hurried over and saw that Marla was in bad shape. "You all right?"

Marla nodded. "I just need..." but she couldn't say another word. She was about to come undone. The waiter looked genuinely concerned.

"What, sweetheart. What do you need?"

Marla pointed to her now empty glass. "Another. And forget the good girl act. Make this one as slutty as you possibly can."

Connie arrived safely in New York. During the taxi ride in from the airport, she stared at the skyline. She was excited, almost like a soldier going into battle.

Marla staggered into her apartment. The bright crimson light on her telephone answering machine blinked hypnotically. She bumped into the furniture on her way to the machine and pushed "play," hating herself for hoping that Zach had left a message, changing his mind. She knew he hadn't. Even drunk, she knew that the phone call wasn't from him.

Connie's recorded voice filled the room. "Something's come up. I'll be out of town for two days. It's a secret, but I can tell you this..." There was playful hesitation. "I've been kidnapped by extra-terrestrials. You'll hear all about the gory details when I get back."

The machine clicked. Marla stared at it unhappily. Oh, she'd wanted it to have been Zach. Not that she had really thought he'd call. There wasn't any way that he would change his mind. But still she'd hoped—

When was she going to learn about men? She tumbled onto the sofa and immediately passed out. Her cat entered the room and climbed onto the pillow next to her. He purred loudly and perched himself on Marla's flat belly, but his mistress didn't even notice.

Marla entered the circle of light. The dream lover was waiting for her, his face hidden in shadow. "Hello, Marla."

She studied the man carefully. "Connie told me about you."

"I know she did. Now, I need you tell me where she is."

"I can't believe you're really here." Marla hesitated.

"Don't feel bad for thinking she was making it all up. Few people would have bought her story. Now, I need you to tell me where she is, so we can clear up a few misunderstandings."

"What do you want with her?"

"I'm the one asking questions, Marla. You're too drunk to even try."

"You want to hurt her."

"Where is she? I can't seem to find her. She can't possibly have been awake for this long."

Marla, tipsy even in her sleep, suddenly giggled. "She's visiting E.T."

"Don't give me that B.S." The ESP lover sprang forward and grabbed Marla in his arms. "Who built the shield?"

In a singsong voice, Marla responded. "Extraterrestrials."

The ESP lover slapped her cheek hard. Marla stopped laughing.

"Who's been protecting the two of you?"

Frightened, but too drunk to hide her emotions, Marla said, "I don't know what you mean."

The man held her even tighter. "God, you don't, do you? She's not telling you anything. Some friend she is."

Marla placed her hand on his crotch and rubbed it up and down. "She did tell me about this, though," she purred. The man, disarmed, let go of Marla's body, and she pushed him just far enough away from her, kneed him in the crotch, and broke out of the room.

Marla leaped from the sofa in total terror. "That's what it was like," she muttered to herself. "Just like Connie said. Breaking free. But that means waking up." She looked down at the cat who eyed her angrily. He didn't appreciate being woken in such a rude manner. Still drunk, Marla tried to stand and crashed into the coffee table. Glasses smashed. A floor lamp tumbled, plunging the room into darkness. Marla was too drunk to realize that she was creating chaos herself, no help needed from Connie's mysterious pursuer. As she struggled to find the light, glass crunched under her foot. She screamed, finally found a light switch, and looked around the room, as if crazed.

"He's here—"

Marla grabbed her keys and ran from the apartment. In the lot, she stumbled to her car, got in, and revved the engine. She put the car into gear and moved off. Immediately, she sideswiped another car. "Oh, damn it."

Not bothering to stop, she careened away from the parked car, grazed another, and drove on. She turned the radio on full blast and began weaving through traffic. Up ahead, Marla saw a cop car with two officers inside. She honked and motioned for the car to pull over. They did, and Marla parked behind, leaving the engine running.

She looked into the mirror, groaned at the sight of her reflection, and ran her fingers through her curls in an attempt to make herself more presentable. One of the cops approached.

"Come on, Marla," she urged herself softly. "Talk slowly. Clearly. Fake it."

The man tapped her window and Marla rolled it down.

"Can I help you, Miss?"

"I'm being chased," Marla said breathlessly.

The cop looked around. The street was empty.

"He's after my friend. After me, too. I don't know what to do."

The cop could smell the alcohol on Marla's breath. "Would you turn off your engine and get out of the car please."

Marla closed her eyes. "He's close. So close. Can't you hear him?"

"Please, Miss?"

She opened her eyes wide, then touched her temples with both hands. "In here. Talking to me."

The cop looked more seriously at her. "Please step out of the car.

We can help you."

"You don't believe me."

The cop tried the door but it was locked. He reached in the window, pulled up the lock, and opened the door. Desperate, Marla put the car into reverse and shot backwards. She pulled back onto the street, nearly hitting the police officer as she accelerated away from the scene.

As she weaved through traffic, a siren sounded behind her. "Oh, my God." Marla said to herself. "What's going to happen? Connie, where are you?"

She sped up, driving her car toward the water, then parked and ran from the car, getting lost in the crowd of tourists out to gaze at the Golden Gate at night. At the end of a pier, she slumped onto a bench. A bum sat at the other end, sucking a beer. "This is my bench," he said.

Marla ignored him, turning to look over her shoulder. She watched the crowd. Her vision became blurred and dark. "Marla," the ESP lover crooned. Marla slapped herself to stay awake. She looked around again, completely paranoid. "He's here," she said softly. "I can't go to sleep. He'll find me. Then he'll find Connie."

"People think I'm nuts," the homeless man said. "But lady—"

Marla twitched as a shiver washed over her. Then she stood and walked to the railing, looking down at the water below. A crazy smiled played over her lips.

"Hey—" the bum called out.

Marla climbed over the railing. People turned and screamed as she fell into the dark water, fifty feet below. A young man ran to the railing, kicked off his shoes, and dove into the water. Someone nearby pulled a fire alarm.

Deleen didn't know what had transpired within her. She also didn't know why she'd pulled the dominatrix routine with Ron. That wasn't like her at all. The concept was simply something that had come to her, an idea pulsing in her mind that refused to be quieted until she'd given in. And seeing Ron like that, helpless, had changed her feelings for him.

Yes, she knew the difference between reality and fantasy, but for some reason, she couldn't get her emotions back to where they'd been before. For the first time since they'd gotten together, she told him she was tired, too tired to make love. Rolling over in the bed, she found herself staring at the wall and wondering if it was too late to change her life.

The heroic man pulled Marla onto the beach. Waiting ambulance workers carried her quickly to safety. Marla was placed on a stretcher and driven to the nearest hospital. She babbled to herself the entire ride, keeping up a steady, incoherent monologue until she was wheeled into the ER.

A doctor bent over Marla, whose eyes were now wide open. She looked totally out of her mind. "You're going to be fine," the doctor said soothingly. He brought out a hypodermic needle. "This is just going to help you sleep."

"No!" Marla screamed. She tried to wrestle the needle from the doctor, but a large male nurse hurried over and held Marla down. The doctor plunged the needle into Marla's arm. "I can't sle—" The doctor smiled, watching the drugs take effect.

"She didn't even get a chance to finish her sentence," the nurse said as Marla's eyes fluttered and closed. "Now, she truly is a sleeping beauty."

The doctor nodded. "Sleeping like a baby. Do I have the touch or what? She'll be out for twelve hours. But God knows if she'll ever get her sanity back."

Inside her mind, Marla was wide awake. She cried helplessly until a soothing voice spoke out to her. "Shhh Marla. He's not here. I won't let him come for you. Just relax, and everything will be okay." Finally, Marla fell peacefully asleep.

# CHAPTER TWENTY-ONE

It was a bad day for Ron Morris.

"I really don't understand," he said as Deleen paced back and forth in his office. She was antsy, ready to flee, and it was obvious from the way she moved that she couldn't wait to get away. Ron took this all in. She had her flight bag packed and was looking at him with an expression he hadn't seen before—not sexy, not happy, not in love with him. Just dead-on serious.

"I guess it was partly the excitement," she said. "The thrill of being naughty, or something. But I really don't think we have a future together."

"You always said—"

"And you said some stuff, too," she reminded him. "Look, maybe it was watching how you treated your wife. Who knows if you'd get tired of me someday and I'd be the one you wouldn't help out. The one pounding on your door in the rain."

"That would never—"

"I don't know why, Ron. I'm just saying that my feelings have changed. And I'm off."

She put her hand out and patted his across the desk. "Best of luck, baby," she said as she exited his office. On her way out the door, she walked by Dick Palmer, the private investigator. He was staring up at the sign on the window that read: Pedal Post. The two passed each other, and Dick took a moment to watch Deleen's fine ass move beneath the tight fabric of her ice blue skirt. Then he headed inside to meet with his employer.

Connie entered the building of a New York television studio skyscraper where she was interviewed by Lyle Patterson. Cameras moved around. The director chose shots. Even two weeks before, this sort of thing would have frightened Connie beyond sensibility. Now, she spoke with calm ease as Patterson quizzed her about her experience. She told him her story with her eyes on his, speaking clearly about even the most difficult details.

"I'm so glad you came to us," Patterson said to her, gripping her hand.

"I just hope this helps," Connie said.

When she was finished, Connie exited the building, finding herself swept along in a river of pedestrians. The flow of bodies stopped at a red light. A huge ad on the side of a bus read: Be Amazed. Watch TAB TV.

Connie looked around as if hearing a voice, but she didn't recognize anyone nearby. The traffic light changed to green and people pushed her into the crosswalk. Connie struggled against the flow, not used to the choreography of pedestrian life in New York. Pedestrians in San Francisco walked to a different beat, not ever so closely packed together.

Reaching the protection of a cafe entrance, she stopped to get her bearings. She seemed to hear the voice again, looked around once more, and then entered the cafe. Finally, all made sense. There was Joseph at a booth. As she joined him, a waitress appeared with a cup of tea that she placed in front of Joseph. He pushed the tea over to Connie, who sipped it with obvious pleasure.

"I really needed this."

"I know."

"I know you know."

"How did the taping go?" Joseph asked.

"I'm sure you saw every second if it from your vantage point at this table."

"I didn't. Because I thought you'd enjoy describing it to me yourself."

"I'm glad you're here," Connie said. "I needed—"

"Sh," Joseph told her, putting one hand on top of hers. "You don't have to say it."

"Why don't I tell you while we window shop. I don't get to New York everyday."

When she'd finished her tea and paid the check, Connie and Joseph found their way along Fifth Avenue, looking into the beautiful windows while she told him about the taping. Connie admired an outfit in the window of Boutique Francaise, an upscale dress shop.

"Try it on," Joseph urged.

"It's probably ten times more than my budget for this whole trip."

"But if you had the money?"

"Sure—"

"Then let's get it. On the way, I'll teach you a few tricks for your boyfriend."

Connie gave Joseph a dirty look.


A bus labeled "Atlantic City Express" moved down the highway. Joseph and Connie sat in the back row, talking softly. They didn't even seem to notice the partying passengers around them. These were people most likely on the way to lose money, yes, but they were also people who still had the chance of walking away winners.

Joseph put his hand over Connie's eyes. She stopped smiling and concentrated. Joseph nodded his head. She was getting the message, getting stronger with each lesson. When she responded to his different prompts, Joseph smiled. Although he wasn't pleased with her plans, he was happy with her progress.

Ron Morris sat stunned at his desk. His mind was consumed by what Deleen had just said. Still, he faced Dick Palmer the private eye Joseph accosted at the airport, waiting to hear the news. Instead of behaving like a hired hand, Dick gave Ron an indignant look, then tossed a bundle of money at him. Ron looked even more bewildered as Dick walked out.

Dick, his money from the winnings at the track still tucked in his pocket, patted his breast pocket reassuringly, and headed toward his car.

At the casino, Joseph and Connie walked passed buzzing, jingling machines towards the card tables where players at a dozen tables peered cautiously at their cards. Connie and Joseph looked around. Joseph indicated several men playing cards at one table. "Pediatricians from Seattle. You want their money?"

Connie shook her head.

Joseph nodded toward a group of aged players. "Retirees from Chicago on a limited income hoping to try their luck."

"Nope."

"Newlyweds?" Joseph asked, jutting his chin toward several happy couples.

"No way," Connie groaned. "They'll have their own problems soon enough."

"That's upbeat," Joseph said, sarcastically, but Connie just shrugged.

Finally, Joseph maneuvered Connie toward the furthest table out, where four tough-looking guys were playing draw poker for serious stakes. Without saying a word, Joseph filled Connie in on the details. "The guy in the white shirt sells cars with unfortunate pedigrees. On his left is someone the DEA would love to talk to.

And the fellow with the stained tie? Biggest slumlord in Pennsylvania."

Connie took a seat at the male-dominated table. Chips were piled high. Joseph sipped a glass of mineral water at the bar across the room. He pretended to watch the action at a table filled with laughing blue-haired ladies. In fact, he had beamed into the heads of the guys at Connie's game. A man wearing an "American Dentist Convention" badge approached Joseph.

"Hey there. I'm Jerry Tucker. You one of us?"

Joseph shook his head. "Nope. I'm a...financial advisor."

He turned toward Connie's table, and in his mind sent her a quick message. "Go for it."

Connie pushed a stack of chips toward the center. "Raise you a thousand."

# CHAPTER TWENTY-TWO

Connie stepped from a dressing room and modeled the outfit that had been displayed in the window for Joseph. She looked dazzling. The dress fit her perfectly, and if she'd always dampened down her beauty in the past, now it shone through fiercely. Connie was a true stunner. "What do you think?"

"What do you think I think?" he teased.

Connie concentrated, receiving his compliments internally. She grinned. "You're sweet," she said. "But are you sure about the shoes?"

He looked down at her feet. Replacing her standard penny loafers, Connie was wearing tall, zippered boots, like the ones she'd had on in several of her fantasies. "Lovely," Joseph said. "They make you look like you're in charge."

After paying, Joseph and Connie exited the shop. She still had her new outfit on, and she and Joseph both carried additional bags. Connie checked her new, expensive watch.

"The show airs in an hour."

"Just enough time to settle in the hotel with a little room service," Joseph smiled. "I'm thinking shrimp cocktail, a bit of caviar..."

"That's not what you're thinking at all," Connie grinned back at him. "No matter how ritzy the place, you're going for a burger tonight."

"That's my girl," Joseph said.

Joseph and Connie sprawled comfortably on the bed in Connie's hotel suite. Still, Connie was nervous.

"Relax," Joseph advised as he clicked on the television. "You've got nothing to do now but wait." Connie nodded and the two watched the set carefully. TAB TV's title clips rolled across the screen. The camera panned to the studio audience, finding the show's host, Lyle Patterson, seated opposite two men. Lyle stared into the camera, his deep brown eyes mesmerizing.

"Do you know what I'm thinking? According to psychic researcher Dr. Carl Trippet..."

The camera focused on Trippet, who fiddled with an EKG monitor. Wires from the device were attached to Trippet's head.

"...Each of us has the potential to read minds." Now, Lyle turned his attention to Sheldon Marks. "On the other hand, Mr. Sheldon Marks, an engineer and member of a group called the Extremely Skeptical People claims ESP doesn't exist. Dr. Trippet, let's begin with you. If ESP actually is real, how does it work?"

"Like all electrical devices, the brain emits energy waves." The doctor threw a switch, and the EKG monitors began to show pictures of his brain waves. "As you all can see, my brain is currently emitting bio-electric impulses. These waves..."

Marks interrupted. "This techno-babble may sound plausible. But there has never been any research that can be scientifically checked, data that can be tested—"

Connie watched the television. Joseph picked up the phone.

"—Simply put, there has never been a single documented case of ESP. Just once in my life, I'd like to see a convincing experiment in the lab. Make me a believer, and I'd be the happiest man on earth. Who wouldn't like to skip all the faxes and email and just mentally hurl our thoughts to one another? Sounds great to me. Maybe it would put the phone company out of business, but I'd be thrilled to sign up as a believer. Until then, I'm the skeptic you've got to win over."

Joseph spoke into the phone. "Room service? Could you send up a burger, medium well, fries, and—" he looked at Connie who said nothing. "A shrimp salad, vinaigrette dressing and a Perrier with a slice of lime."

Marla watched TAB TV on her sofa, her pet cat right next to her.
"A lab isn't the only place to find the truth," Trippet said.
"But it's the only place to prove it," Marks retorted.

Connie looked disgusted. With a violent stab at the remote control, she muted the TV, talking to the set with her back toward Joseph. "This Marks is so smug. I'd like to tell him a thing or two." She paused, "Unless—"

Suddenly, an idea occurred to her. Behind her, Joseph grinned. Unbeknownst to Connie, he was mentally feeding her this concept.

"What if this guy Marks is working for the government's ESP project? Those folks aren't eager to have the masses believe this stuff. He could be part of a set-up. In fact," she paused again, working a possible situation out in her mind. "In fact, they both could be in on the same scam. Trippet looks like a total loon with his wires and his psychobabble. And this guy Marks comes across as reasonable and steady. They could be in cahoots to fool the general public into believing that ESP is just a crock for crazy people."

She was pleased with this conspiracy notion until she turned to Joseph. Seeing him smiling at her, she realized this was his idea all along. "Joseph," she said, giggling. "You're awful." Then she turned back to the TV, unmuting it.

"We'll put the debate aside to hear from someone who had a sexy ESP experience firsthand. Right after these messages."

An advertisement began to play.

As Marla used the commercial break to get a snack, the kitchen phone rang. She nestled the receiver against her ear as she assembled a sandwich. "No, she's not here, Ron. Nope, I don't have a clue where she is. And you know what?" she took a deep breath preparing to say something that would give her great joy. "I wouldn't tell you if I did know because you pushed her out on the street, you sadistic son of a bitch." Marla slammed down the phone, smiling with satisfaction.

The phone rang again, almost immediately, but Marla just made a face at it, unwilling to further engage in a phone battle with Connie's husband.

After gathering her snack, she returned to the living room. The words "taped earlier" appeared on the bottom of the screen. Lyle began talking. "For reasons that will soon become clear, it has been necessary to disguise our next guest's voice and appearance and to give her a pseudonym." The camera pulled back to reveal Connie's face, which had been electronically distorted by tiny colorful squares.

Lyle continued in a soothing voice. "Ellen, please tell us your story."

When Connie spoke, her voice was oddly mechanical sounding, like that of a robot. "A month ago, I was in bed reading."

Marla got comfortable on the sofa and began eating her sandwich. On the television, a lovely blonde actress, about Connie's age, curled in bed reading a romance novel. She was dressed in a leopard-print nightie that looked like something right out of Marla's closet—but about the last thing on earth Connie would wear. Her full breasts spilled over the lacy bodice and her cherry-glossed lips pursed dramatically as she read the steamy words on the page of her novel. After a moment she fanned herself with the open novel, as if she were growing hotter with each word.

The word "dramatization" briefly appeared on the screen. As the woman reenacted the scene, Connie narrated. "Soon, I fell asleep. But it was the most unusual sleep of my life. I found myself in this strange, empty place. A dark bare room lit eerily from above. Honestly, this didn't feel like a dream at all. It felt as if I had entered a real room. Something that existed somewhere far from my home."

Marla was stunned when she realized that she was listening to Connie's story. She perched on the edge of her sofa, the sandwich in one hand forgotten.

Connie viewed the same show with similar intensity. Hearing her own story played back to her was disconcerting. Joseph didn't appear to share her interest. Instead, he focused on the fact that someone was approaching the door. Quickly, he took money from his wallet just as the room service man was about to knock. Joseph handed the man the cash and took the tray. Then he glanced over at the television set.

On the TV, Connie's look-alike entered an area that resembled the mental scenario where she had met the ESP lover, except that this place was decorated far more Hollywood-style. Sumptuous sapphire fabric draped the walls and the floor glittered with sparkling diamond dust.

Connie, with her voice distorted, continued to describe the action like a play-by-play. "Then a man appeared. He was tall and lean, and although I tried to figure out who he was, I couldn't see his face."

An actor playing the ESP lover emerged from the shadows. His face was hidden by the type of black nylon mask favored by bank robbers.

"He beckoned me to come toward him, and I refused."

The actor playing the ESP lover walked toward the actress playing Connie. The woman turned away and put up one hand dramatically to stop him. She looked like an erotic traffic cop.

"He took me in his arms and held me tightly. I told him that I was married. He said, 'That bond means nothing here. Your husband won't find out about what we've done together. Give in and enjoy yourself.' I struggled and ran away."

Still on the TV, the focus returned to the interview between Lyle and Connie. Her voice continued to be distorted throughout their conversation. "Why did you run?"

"Because I don't like to be manipulated."

"What happened next?" the host urged.

"The very next night, I found myself back in that strange place, only now there was a bed and flowers. Candles were lit. Music played softly. It was a scene made for romance, and that's precisely what this man had planned for us. When he spoke to me, he made it clear that he knew things that I like. Things that I've never even told anyone that I wanted."

"This ESP lover must have read your mind."

The actor sat on the bed. The actress playing Connie moved toward him. "Although I couldn't see his real face, he was incredibly attractive to me. I went to him in spite of myself."

The dramatization continued. The ESP lover and the actress playing Connie fell into bed. They kissed passionately as the man began to remove the woman's clothes. Details were hidden by discreet camera angles, but the scene remained plenty passionate, especially due to the soft moans of the hired players.

"It was the most beautiful love-making of my life," Connie's off-screen voice declared. "I've never experienced anything so earth-shaking." Another hesitation. "Not even with my husband. I know there are skeptics out there who won't believe my story. People who will say that I made it all up. But I didn't. If you'd experienced what I've experienced, then you'd know how amazing it could be."

The camera now focused back on Lyle and Connie. "What we need to know is why you came forward with this story, Ellen. Why now?"

Though the electronic distortion made it difficult to tell for sure,

Connie appeared to be wiping away her tears. "After we made love, he came to me several more times. Each night that my husband was away on his business trip, we formed a strong erotic connection. But then he stopped. I must have said something or done something that drove him away, although I can't figure out what I did. I've tried to go on with my life, but I'm unable. He is all I think about, all that I desire. Now I want one more chance to tell him how I really feel."

In the hotel room, Joseph smiled at Connie. "No self-respecting ESP lover would be able to resist that sort of heartfelt appeal."

"I'm not going after his heart, Joseph—"

Back on the TV, Lyle faced Connie. "Couldn't you just signal him by ESP? Show up in his mind wearing an imaginary nightie and make-believe high-heeled slippers? Take it from me, guys like a forward woman every now and again."

"My psychic powers are limited. In my quest to find him again, I've done a little bit of research, and I've learned that I am what you'd call a 'receiver,' not a 'sender.' I can welcome him into my head, but I can't get into his. Your show was the only way I could think of to contact him."

Now, Lyle looked directly into the camera. "This might be the world's first instance of an ESP dating service." Facing Connie again he said, "We'd like you to come back again and visit us. Let us know how it works out."

The interview with Connie faded out, replaced by a shot of Lyle sitting with Trippet and Marks. "We're back live, gentlemen. I want each of you to comment on this extraordinary story. Then we'll give our viewers across the country their chance to call in—or send us emails. And, of course, any ESP lovers can just beam their comments directly to my brain. But first, these commercial messages."

In Connie's hotel room, she switched off the television and glanced at the digital clock by the bed. It was 10:30. She started to pace nervously, her bare feet wearing treads into the richly napped burgundy carpet.

"He's not going to burst in here like a robber, Connie. You have

231

to wait. Didn't you ever go fishing?"

Connie shook her head. "But I'm sure you're an ace angler. You seem the type. Calm and patient—"

Joseph nodded. "That's why I was in the sporting goods store the day Madame Largo came to buy her gun."

Connie paced again and then walked over to the window. She gazed out at the Manhattan skyline, alive with twinkling lights. Joseph stared at her, picking up one of her thoughts. "No. It would not be best if you met him alone. He's dangerous Connie. He tried to go after Marla when he couldn't find you." Connie continued to carry on her side of the conversation via ESP.

"Forget that two's company nonsense. He won't even know I'm here. I can hide much better than he can. He hasn't sensed my presence yet, has he? Not even the night you got drunk. I have experience with this sort of thing. Far more than you have."

Connie turned now and stared fiercely at Joseph. Her green eyes glowed.

"Forget it. It's too dangerous. I won't let him hurt you."

She widened her eyes.

"You don't have to yell," Joseph sighed. When Connie silently disagreed with the statement he said, "Yes, you were too yelling."

Finally, Connie sat down on one of the deep leather chairs in the room. "It's my life and my dream lover. I know what I'm doing."

"Do you?"

"You won't always be with me, Joseph. You're going to have to have faith in your own ability as a teacher at some point. Faith in me, too. Do you think you can believe in me?"

Joseph gave her a look, and then headed for the door. She smiled gratefully at his back.

"You're welcome," Joseph said. Then he exited. Connie closed the door and locked it. Then she leaned against the wood, deep in thought.

Marla watched TAB TV. On the screen, as Trippet and Marks debated Connie's presentation, the toll-free number was once again superimposed over the guests. 1-888-AMAZING.

"What a sensational love story," Trippet gushed.

"The word I'd use is unbelievable,'" Marks snorted.

"Let's see what our viewers think," Lyle interrupted. "Mary from Boise, you're on TAB TV."

"This is the devil's work," the caller insisted vehemently. "And you're assisting Satan by allowing this woman to appear on your program. You should be ashamed."

"I'd advise you to turn off your TV," Lyle snapped.

There was a knock on Marla's door. She muted the television and went to answer.

In the luxurious hotel bathroom, Connie soaked in a bubble-filled tub. Several perfumed candles sent their soothing fragrance into the atmosphere. Connie needed all the relaxation techniques she could get. Inside, she felt as anxious as she'd ever been. Yet, beneath that wave of nervousness, she knew that she was strong.

Joseph walked the streets of New York, staying close by the hotel. He was deep in thought.

Connie lay in bed staring up at the ceiling. She seemed to be preparing herself mentally for a big event. Her lips were pressed firmly together and her eyes held an unflinching gaze. Finally, she turned out the light.

Joseph continued to walk.

Connie closed her eyes.

"I'm with you," Joseph told her in her head. "Don't be scared."

"Do you remember me?" the man asked.

Marla stared trying to figure out who this was. He was handsome. About her age, with reddish hair and dark brown eyes the color of a Fudgsicle. She'd remember meeting him before, wouldn't she? Like she'd told Connie, she generally kept a running tab of men she'd flirted with.

"Look, I don't want to frighten you. It's just that I can't stop thinking about you."

And then she got it. This was the man who'd rescued her, the one who jumped into the water after she'd taken the dive off the pier. "I read your name in the paper," he said, trying to explain. "Looked you up. But you didn't answer the phone, so I thought I'd come by and give you these."

He held out a beautiful bouquet of flowers.

Marla sneezed immediately, allergic to them.

"Oh, God, I'm sorry—" the man said, watching Marla wipe at her eyes.

"You couldn't have known," she said, watching him toss the flowers away from himself. She spoke the words with relief. Connie's dream lover would have been able to read her mind, to know that she couldn't take any sort of live flower. So she knew this wasn't the dream lover, wasn't someone who could read her mind at all. But she had one more thing she needed to know.

"You're not a musician, are you?" she asked, hand still on the chain lock.

He shook his head. "I teach over at SFSU. Sorry. Do you only date musicians?"

Quickly, Marla undid the chain. "Nope," she grinned, opening the door. "I only date professors at SFSU."

Connie slept in her bed. As soon as she faded into her dreams, she entered the mind set. It looked exactly as it had during the initial seduction scene. The dream lover sat on the bed. His face remained shielded. Connie emerged from the shadows. She looked magnificent, like a well-rehearsed actress returning to Broadway.

"Hello, Connie."

"It's you—" she said, surprised within herself that her plan had actually worked.

"Who else knows how to find this place? Besides, you invited me."

"Yes, I did."

"Come closer."

Connie moved toward the bed.

"Shall we make love again? I've got the ties—"

"Show me your face."

"I can't do that."

"Actually, I don't need your permission." A narrow beam of light fell into the center of the man's face. He threw his hand upward to fend it off, but like an X-ray, the light pierced his palm.

"What are you doing?!"

Joseph sat on a marble bench near the hotel. His eyes were closed. He smiled.

In the mind set, the golden beam of light slowly expanded, revealing the man's lips, then his eyes then his entire face. The lover tried to cover his identity with his arms, but he failed to hide himself from Connie's strengthened power.

"Show me your face," Connie repeated sternly.

When the man shook his head his arms were thrown apart by an invisible force. Connie squinted her eyes, looking at him. His face closely resembled the face in the drawing made during Connie's visit with Dr. Peters, but there was no big revelation in Connie's mind. She'd thought that seeing him again would somehow clear things up for her. No such luck—the man was still a stranger. Connie moved closer. "I don't get it. I still don't know you. I was sure that if I saw you for real, I mean, in this place, I would know who you are. Tell me your name."

"I won't."

"You will."

The man remained silent, blue eyes blazing. Connie steadily approached him.

"Your name."

The man said nothing.

"Now!"

The ESP lover seemed to shrink physically as Connie grew closer.

"Don't make me tell. They'll banish me from the project."

"Your project means nothing to me."

"If you knew about it, you wouldn't say that. We're working for the nation's security. For the good of all America."

"How does destroying my life fit into that?"

The man looked down. Connie focused all of her energy on the man, utilizing every lesson she'd learned from Joseph. The man closed his eyes, trying to keep her out of his consciousness in a losing mental battle. Then slowly, his eyes opened. "My name is Jason Fowler."

Connie continued to stare into his eyes.

"That's right. You haven't heard my name before. You don't know me. But I know you, thanks to Deleen. My soon-to-be-ex wife."

Joseph sat quietly listening.

Connie circled the ESP lover like a fighter.

"We'd been married two years. Just like all the other wives and husbands of members in this program, Deleen had no idea that I was involved in psychic research. She thought I was a computer programmer. Everyone on our team signs a pledge not to discuss the work outside the lab, and not to use the power for any sort of personal gain. I honored that pledge scrupulously. At least, at first." He sighed, and looked up at Connie and she saw a strange vulnerability in his eyes.

"Go on—"

"One day I came home and found Deleen wearing a smile more radiant than any I had ever seen. It floored me. I mean, I'm a man. I've got instincts that have nothing to do with the power. I knew immediately that something was different about her. Instead of asking questions, the way I suppose a normal husband would, I decided to see for myself exactly what had put that smile on her face." Again he sighed, "Look, I know it was wrong, but I couldn't help myself. Anyone in my position would have done the same thing. If she'd been innocent, then maybe I would have felt a little guilty for probing her mental cupboards. But she wasn't. That night, I learned that it wasn't me who was making her glow. The delight on her face came from the memory of sex she had just had with another man. With a man you know well, Connie."

She just stared at him, confused.

"Come on, Connie. Pick up the clues here. You're not stupid. I've been in your head long enough to know that. You're just trusting and naive, two qualities that are extremely appealing but tend to set you back. I'll spell it out for you if you need me to—Deleen had been sleeping with your husband Ron."

"No," Connie said. "You should have seen how upset he was when he thought *I* was cheating. There's no way that Ron would ever—"

"You wouldn't be nearly so shocked if you could read your husband's mind the way I read Deleen's."

"I don't believe you—"

"But that's not actually true, is it, Connie? It's not that you don't believe—it's that you don't *want* to believe. There's a big difference. Remember the diamond earrings he gave you for your last birthday? Those were supposed to go to Deleen. You found them accidentally, and he had to hand them over to save face. But later, when you weren't home, he brought those beauties to a jeweler who took real diamonds out and had them replaced with fakes—hose zirconium things. He gave the real ones to my wife. They looked stunning on her, when she had them on, and nothing else—"

"But I don't understand," Connie said.

"Which part? It's all very clear when you have all the facts."

"I don't understand why you kept coming back. Why you played me the way you did." She thought about the different times with him—the erotic visions they'd shared. How could she have had such an intense connection with someone whose only desire was revenge?

The dream lover read her mind easily. He half-smiled at her, then shrugged. "It was too much of a temptation not to. It had been a long time since I'd last been with someone new. Someone who I could so easily please. There you were with your fantasies all spread out for me like some delicious feast. I couldn't help myself. I felt as if you needed me. Yeah, I used you, Connie. But didn't I help, as well? Didn't I change your world for the better?"

Joseph sat still as before, but he no longer smiled. Across the street, a drunken couple staggered out of a club. They made their way up to a motor scooter and, giggling, climbed on it with some difficulty. The man attempted to start the machine without success.

"Damn it."

"Must have a thing against drunk drivers!"

"I'm not drunk. Just got a little buzz on."

Connie covered her ears and shook her head as the ESP lover

poured out the truth. "I probed deeper and learned that your husband and my wife had met many times while I was in the lab and while you were teaching those innocent school kids. She's a first class flight attendant. The opportunities were endless for them. They met on one of his trips, Connie. And now he travels with her on his business excursions. And he's not always on business trips when he goes away."

"Why didn't you just divorce her? Why did you come after me?"

"I couldn't let her get away with that. I needed payback."

"So to get your revenge, you ruined my life?"

The man shrugged. "It was already ruined, wasn't it? You just didn't know."

"That makes it right?"

"It should make it more bearable. Would you really have wanted to stay with someone who was treating you the way Ron was? He took you for granted, Connie. Deleen wasn't the first woman he'd been with."

"You've been in his head, too?"

"Of course."

"Then why would you go after me? Why wouldn't you have attacked him directly?"

"Because he has an ego like none other. The worst thing I could do to him was woo you away. He believed fully in his powers of keeping you contained. Neatly boxed up in his own vision of you. Breaking you out of that, and making you cheat on him, that was the way for me to truly rock his foundation."

Joseph continued to sit and concentrate. All of his mental powers were focused on what was going on in Connie's mind. Across the street, the drunks finally got their scooter working. The vehicle leapt forward, turned in a circle, and screeched out of control, directly toward Joseph. He saw it coming, but didn't have time to avoid the machine, which crashed into him, knocking him to the ground.

Still in the mind set, Connie sensed the accident at the second of impact. She was jolted as if she'd been the one hit, and she turned away as if looking at a scene somewhere else. "Oh, my God! Joseph."

Her momentary loss of focus allowed the ESP lover to temporarily regain his strength. He'd been waiting for a second chance, a moment to regroup. Now that he had it, his skin appeared to shine. He looked bigger, more imposing. He sprinted after Connie.

"Stop!" The force of his voice knocked Connie to her knees. The man towered over her, his anger tangible. "Who taught you how to penetrate my mask?"

"You'll never know," Connie said weakly. The man continued to grow larger and more threatening.

"We need him for our work."

"But you can't have him," Connie whispered. "I won't let you."

"I need to meet this...Joseph."

Connie struggled to her feet. With a wave of his hand, the man knocked her back down. She rolled on the floor.

"Do you want to be mental vegetable forever, babbling in some corner of a dingy hospital?" he asked. Then his voice lowered. "I can turn off the light inside you, Connie. Do you want to die to protect him?"

She crawled toward the safety of the shadows. Psychically, he drew her back. Her fingers clutched for purchase on the wood floor, but found nothing. She slid closer to him. "You can't escape, Connie. Your only ability to save yourself is to bring him to me. Now."

Joseph lay flat on his back. Several passersby hurried to his aid.

One was a doctor, who quickly checked Joseph's pulse and saw that he was still breathing, just battered. The two drunks sat on the ground nearby, frightened. In the distance, a siren sounded. The doctor bent close to Joseph. "Can you hear me, Sir?"

"Don't give in, Connie—"

The ESP Lover had pulled Connie to her feet.

"Connie, stay focused," Joseph murmured. "Be strong. You know what you have to do."

The man looked around, hearing Joseph's voice, but unable to see him. "Where is he Connie? Call him to you."

"Keep away, Joe. I'm fine," Connie insisted. To the lover she said, "You're lucky that he's not here. But let me show you one of his better tricks." Connie stared into the man's eyes. He stared back, obviously no longer afraid of her. Suddenly, she disappeared. The man looked around, confused. "Where'd you go?"

"I thought you liked to play hide-and-seek. Didn't you tell me that once? Weren't you the master of this game?"

The man turned and looked for her. "Come back!"

Connie, unseen but in a place behind him, taunted, "Over here."

"Where?"

Connie could be seen only in a stroboscopic flash of light. She pummeled the man, driving him to the ground. He pushed himself up. She crushed him again. He got to his knees. She smashed him, psychically hitting him again and again. Finally, he lay there, beaten, whimpering.

"Do you still want to see the man who taught me? He won't be quite so gentle with you, I can assure you of that."

The man shook his head slowly.

"Now," Connie said, "What's my name?"

"It's... It's..." he didn't know.

"Just like a man. How soon they forget. And what's my teacher's name?"

"I don't know."

"But you just heard it."

"I don't know."

"Where do I live?"

He shook his head. "I..."

"What do I look like?"

The ESP lover assumed the fetal position, holding his head to keep it from exploding.

"This has been a bad dream. When you wake up, you'll remember none of it."

Utterly vanquished, the man crawled off toward the shadows.

"Go play your mind games, Jason. But don't come back!"

The man disappeared into the dark.

# CHAPTER TWENTY-THREE

Joseph was being attended to by the doctor and several paramedics. A pair of uniformed police officers had taken the drunken couple into custody.

"Let's get you to the hospital, sir," one of the paramedics said.

"I'm okay. Just had the wind knocked out of me."

In his mind, Connie called out to him, "Joseph, are you all right?"

"Yes," he murmured.

"We have to take you in just to check everything out."

"Thanks, but no thanks."

The paramedics helped Joseph to stand and then began to move him to the waiting ambulance. "Trust us, sir. We know what's best. When you're knocked down like that, you could have a multitude of problems that won't immediately be apparent. A concussion, internal bruising or bleeding. Our doctors can make an assessment."

Joseph pulled free. Before the paramedic could grab him, the second paramedic intervened. "I think he's okay."

"What are you talking about? The guy's out on his feet."

"Let him go. He's fine," the doctor added.

"Are you both nuts? This man just was run over by a..." Joseph focused on the paramedic. "I guess you guys are right. He's okay. He's great."

*"Joseph, stop manipulating them. You ought to go to the hospital."*

"I have a better idea," Joseph mentally told Connie. "Let's go home."

"Are you really okay?"

He answered her in the affirmative.

"Then I have an even better idea," Connie said, "Why don't you get yourself back to the hotel—"

"You wanted to tell me something," Connie whispered. "You have for a long time. Maybe since we first met."

"Yes—"

"But I felt you holding back. In the airport. And some other times, too."

"You weren't ready," Joseph said. "There were too many unanswered questions in your mind, too many loose ends. It wasn't the right time."

"I'm ready now."

He came forward, taking her in his arms and holding tight. "Do I have to say it?"

Connie looked into his eyes. Gray-blue, ever changing. She saw there what she'd failed to see over his month of teaching her. He loved her. Was that true?

He nodded, having easily read the question in her mind. And he could also read the answer there, as well.

They moved together as they had on the dance floor,

hesitatingly, slowly. At first, it was awkward. She knew exactly what he was thinking—he knew what she was thinking. There was none of that innocent fumbling that characterizes most first-times. And yet, Connie found that she actually missed the innocence. Worse than that, within herself, she felt guilty when she realized that Joseph knew each and every action she'd performed with the ESP lover. He knew about her striptease and the outdoor sex. He knew everything.

"Stop worrying," Joseph said, and his voice was out loud rather than in her head, startling her.

"I'm sorry—"

"And don't be sorry," he said. "Here's the thing—what you did with him doesn't count. It was like screwing with a hologram, with a piece of fabricated fluff. Being jealous of that would be like being jealous of a teenage girl's crush on a movie star. Sure, it might have been sexy to have a lover who could literally read your mind. But what's even sexier is learning for yourself. So stop thinking, and just let go."

As Joseph spoke, Connie felt herself relax. She looked up at him and then took his hand and placed it on her body. Her fingers overlapped with his; she showed him how she most liked to be touched. Gently at first, softly, until the heat began to build within her. Joseph reciprocated immediately, becoming an almost instant master at giving her pleasure. He stroked his fingertips under her heavy mane of hair, spread his warm hands over her shoulders, working them slowly down lower and lower.

Connie sighed at the thrill of it. Spurred on by her reaction, Joseph continued. His fingers found the slippery wet split of her body and he parted her lips and slid his fingertips against her. He learned from her responses exactly the way to touch her, and for the first time in real life, Connie was able to let loose. This wasn't in her head. This was in a real, man-made bed.

"Oh, yes—" Connie moaned. "That's right."

Tantalizing circles skimmed over that most secret part of her, and she gripped Joseph's shoulders. When she looked into his face, his outline held steady for her. She could see what he really looked like. No blurred vision, no transformations. This was the real Joseph—n the flesh, without the assistance of his powers to cloud her mind, to make her vision blurry. The realness of his body, the warmth of his skin, smell of his hair, turned Connie on more than anything she could remember.

In a flash she understood a lesson that the dream lover had never wanted her to know—reality was worlds better than make-believe.

# CHAPTER TWENTY-FOUR

Joseph and Connie sat side by side on an airplane. First class, of course, thanks to their recent Atlantic City success. While Joseph shut his eyes, Connie spoke into an Airfone. "I know you don't want to have anything to do with him. But you can just tell him its flight 65. Then you can tell me all about doing the professor, you naughty school girl, you."

As she hung up, the plane was jolted by an air pocket.

"Ladies and gentlemen," the attendant announced. "Because of the turbulence, the captain has turned on the seat belt sign. If you are up and about the cabin, please return to your seats now."

"I guess that's it for the mile high club," Joseph sighed.

"I hate flying. And this bouncing around doesn't help."

"You'd be even more frightened if you knew what the pilots were thinking right now."

Connie froze.

"Just kidding."

She took a deep breath. "Maybe I wouldn't want to be inside the pilot's head, but when I look around and see people's faces, they always look so interesting. I wish I could do some quick mental eavesdropping. I know my powers have grown, but I'm not nearly at the level that you are."

"Do you really want to know?"

She nodded, looking over at a businessman across the aisle. Immediately, she could see into his mind, as he mentally went over the firing of a pleading employee. And then, as she gazed around the plane, she could peer into each person's mind. With Joseph's help, Connie saw it all. Some embarrassing thoughts, some sexy, some scary, some tender. She found the knowledge noisy and overwhelming. Ultimately, the content didn't matter. It was the medium itself, the violation of privacy, that made this type of voyeurism too much for Connie.

"My mom always told me, be careful what you wish for."

"Marla said the same thing."

Joseph patted her hand.


Connie and Joseph stood at the baggage carrousel. She struggled with one of her bags as her husband walked up and helped her to lift it. "Hello, Ron," she said. Then as a reflex, she almost introduced Ron to Joseph, who stood next to her, but she caught herself.

"I got your message," Ron said.

"Marla told me you were looking for me."

Ron noticed Joseph standing so close by and he whispered to Connie that he wanted to talk to her away from the homeless man. She smiled slightly and followed him a few steps away. Joseph was at his old tricks again, blurring Ron's vision of him.

"What have you been up to?" Ron asked.

"One thing and another."

"What sort of answer is that?"

"Enough of one."

Ron gave her a fierce look. She returned it and more, putting into her gaze a fraction of the same power she'd used to vanquish his girlfriend's husband. When he saw that he couldn't make her back down, his expression softened. "Look, honey, I don't want us to be apart." He waited for her response, but got nothing. "We could resolve this thing in a second. Just explain what happened in that motel."

"Isn't there a story you ought to be telling me instead? Isn't there a whole novel you should be confessing to?"

He stared at her, sensing that she somehow knew everything about his trysts. Then he stood silent, looking for the courage to open up, but ultimately, he couldn't. Connie nodded. She'd expected as much. Reaching into the side pocket of her purse, she removed her wedding band and engagement ring and handed both over. He said nothing as he palmed the jewelry, and then shaking his head slowly walked away.

"Maybe some other time," Connie said softly. After a moment, she approached Joseph. "I suppose you heard all that?"

He nodded.

"I wonder if he'll ever come clean with me. Just to heal his soul, and all that."

"I'm not a fortune teller."

Connie put her luggage on a cart. The two headed to the exit. Connie pointed to the parking garage across the way. "My car's there."

"I know."

A flurry of other passengers surrounded the couple. For a second, Connie heard all of their thoughts. She glanced up at Joseph, confused. Why was he letting her eavesdrop again? Then he put his arms around her and whispered, "But Connie, here's one that won't make you sad—tell me now, what am I thinking?"

# EPILOGUE

"I want to play," he said, sliding her white sweats down her thighs. Connie nodded and reached her hands above her head as he pulled her shirt off her. She had an idea what he was going to do, but she didn't ask him. That was part of the fun. No mind reading was allowed in their bedroom. Everything unfolded naturally, step by step. He told her to lie down on a long, low table. While she made herself as comfortable as she could, he said, "Close your eyes." She stared up at him, until he said, "trust me."

She heard him say those two words in her head again: *Trust me*. Then she shut her eyes, but she couldn't keep herself from trembling. They were in Joseph's studio. It wasn't in her mind. It was in a real room. So different from the mental games the dream lover had played. When Joseph wanted to push her boundaries, he did so in real life.

Now Joseph perched on the edge of the table. He looked Connie over before he started, then glanced back at the materials. The colorful bottles of edible paint were lined up on the floor. He reached for the purple one, dipped in a brush, and began to draw spirals on Connie's slender thighs. She shook slightly at the cold sensation, but she kept her eyes closed. He could tell from her expression that she was trying not to laugh.

"Does it tickle?"

She made a sound deep in her throat, a low murmur. He took it for an assent, but he didn't stop painting. He didn't care if she moved, the motion added to the designs. When he was done with the purple, he reached for red. Her skin made the perfect canvas, so pale that the colors really stood out against it. Connie's thick blonde hair and pale complexion made her look like Sleeping Beauty.

She opened her eyes as Joseph put the red paint down and reached for a bottle of gold. He drew stripes on her arms, making her look sort of tribal. Purposefully, he avoided her small breasts, even though he could tell that she was arching slightly, hoping he'd paint them. He didn't come close to her inner thighs either, not wanting to start the sex until he was finished with his art.

Connie stared at him, smiling. "You can see everything, can't you?"

He nodded, intent on his work. "This was just a fleeting image you had last year," he said. "You wanted someone to turn you into a work of art. I know, Connie. I know everything."

She sighed. It was reassuring, somehow, to hear someone say that. And to have the person not be shocked by what he saw in her mind. She'd never been this open with anyone. Definitely not Ron, and not even Marla, who she was pretty certain would never judge her, and not even with the dream lover. There had been fantasies he'd found, and fantasies that remained hidden until she'd invited Joseph to peruse the X-rated files of her mind.

Moving slowly along the table toward Connie, he took her in his arms and brought his mouth to hers, kissing her. His lips were soft, his fingers finding the ribbon in Connie's hair and pulling it free, letting her golden curls spill down her back. Connie trembled in his embrace. Then he gently released her and picked up something new—a bottle Connie couldn't see.

"What's that?" she murmured.

"Honey—"

Dipping a fresh paintbrush into the jar, he coated it with the sugary syrup. Connie closed her eyes as Joseph drew one long line down the center of her body. The brush tickled and the sticky sap clung to her skin. He brought his mouth to the painted line and licked it, smiling as he said, "sweet." Then he returned to painting. He drew concentric circles around Connie's nipples. They were erect, pointing upward, and Connie trembled as the honey coated them.

Joseph painted Connie's ribs, painted along her pubic bone. "I love the way the honey looks against your skin," he murmured. "Glistening and wet, like liquid amber." Then he set the brush aside.

Connie's body started to shake as he pressed his lips to her flat stomach and began to lick, lapping deliciously at the thick spill of honey. Connie relaxed and closed her eyes. Joseph caressed her with his fingertips, finding just the right way to touch her. His knowing tongue quickly began making the darting little circles that Connie loved best. He went around and around with the tip of his tongue, and Connie slid on the cool table, arching her hips upward, helping him. She tensed her muscles, getting closer....

Then everything stopped.

Connie opened her eyes, startled. Joseph sat on his heels, regarding her, not saying a word.

Connie swallowed hard, waiting.

"So you want to be my canvas?" he asked, his voice gone dark and low and sweet.

She leaned her head back against the bench, her whole body straining. "Yes," she finally managed.

"Then I'm going to choose the medium with which I paint you."

"Yes," she agreed, "whatever you want. However you want it."

Again, he kissed her. His mouth was sweet, his lips curved into a smile even as his tongue met Connie's. His kisses made her moan out loud. Connie's body pressed against his, slid against his, sticky and hot.

"Slowly," Joseph said, his fingers drawing designs in the honey on her body. She trembled at his touch. "Slowly," he whispered, and his eyes glowed fiercely, showing Connie everything, one brush stroke before it happened.

And then he undid his faded jeans and with Connie's eyes wide open and watching, he slid forward, pressing into her, *finally* pressing into her. She was joined to him, joined with sex and sweet clover-scented honey. Joseph held onto her shoulders, his fingers sliding in the honey, his body sliding against hers. He held Connie as the waves washed over her. Then he pulled out, mixing the juices of their sex with the honey. He painted Connie with *this*. With sex. Her skin was his canvas. And as he painted her, he created her anew. Turned her into a work of art.

A masterpiece.